EMP

By Wilson Harp

Table of Contents

ONE

The 108 turnoff had always been tricky for folks who came out to visit us. The new four-lane made it easier to see, but it would still sneak up on you if you weren't expecting it around the bend.

For me, it was all the same. I had made that turn off the main highway as long as I had been driving. I had known the shift and speed of the car as it made that turn since the time I was old enough to stand in the back seat and watch for deer along the woods as we came home from a trip to town.

Right now I was just frustrated with the radio as I came upon the turn. Every station out here was either country or local talk. My satellite radio was out of service and my MP3 device was in the trunk in the side pocket of my gym bag. I found an NPR station out of Rolla and was listening to some boring report about some solar flare that was going to happen soon.

Boring, to me at least, the physicist they were interviewing was very excited. But between the subject matter and the fact that the signal kept cutting out, I decided to just turn it off.

I was almost home anyway. Well, it felt like home. Kenton was the town I was born and raised in. Technically, I was born in Poplar Bluff, but my folks took me back to Kenton when I was three days old.

The place where I currently lived was Oak Park just outside Chicago. Currently was the key word. I wasn't sure what Lexi would decide this weekend. Things had been rough the last few months. I wasn't sure what she wanted, apart from space and her need to sort things out. What things, were a total mystery to me.

My cell phone rang and I reached up and hit the earpiece.

"Hello," I said.

"David, are you on the road?" My mom's voice sounded frustrated.

"Yeah, I'm on the road mom. About five miles from town."

"Did you pull over to answer the phone?"

"No, still driving."

"You shouldn't answer the phone while you're driving. That's dangerous. Pull over right now."

I did not pull over. The thought went through my head to tell her if it was so dangerous for me to talk while driving, then perhaps she shouldn't call while she knows I am traveling. I resisted the impulse.

"Okay, Mom. Pulled over. What's up?"

"I just wanted to remind you to pick up the medicine at the drug store."

"Okay. Just Dad's prescription?"

"Yes. And it's the white pharmacy, not Turner's."

Turner's pharmacy had been closed for close to twenty years now. Mom was getting worse.

"Okay Mom. I'll pick it up."

"Thank you. And we are having green beans for dinner with some of those fresh tomatoes your father picked yesterday."

It was early April, the tomato plants in the garden had barely started coming up. Dad must have picked some up at the store yesterday.

"Sounds great, Mom. See you in a little while."

"Okay, David. We'll see you soon. Love you."

"Love you, too, Mom."

I hung up the phone as I turned onto Dyer Street. I still expected the whine of the tires to change as I moved from the blacktop highway to the city street. It had always been that way growing up. But, all of the roads had been smoothed and resurfaced many times since then.

Turner's pharmacy was now a woman's clothing store on the corner of Main and Dyer. Hanson's pharmacy was what most people referred to as the white pharmacy. Hanson had bad luck with his new sign when he opened. Lost it three times the first two months. He decided he was better off just leaving it down. His white building along a row of brick storefronts on Main stuck out like a sore thumb. There was no need for a sign anymore, though the bags still said Hanson's Pharmacy.

A spot out front was open and I parked the car. Not as much traffic as I remember, but downtown hasn't been the same for a long time. The new Wal-Mart in Wilcox has sucked away most of the day to day shopping. Kenton was a quintessential dying small town. Every generation seemed to get restless to move on, and while there were a few locals who had deep roots to the town, much of the new population were people trying to escape to the idealized, idyllic country life.

I got out of my car and walked to the glass door of the pharmacy. A tinkling bell alerted everyone inside that someone had entered.

"Well, Dave Hartsman! How are you?" Sue Parnell was the oldest sister of one of my buddies from High School. She was Sue Hanson now. She came over and gave me a hug.

"Hi Sue, doing good. How are you and Billy?" I asked.

"We're doing good. Is Lexi here?" she asked as she looked out at my car.

"No, Emma had a school thing so they stayed up in Chicago this weekend."

"Dave," Billy called as he saw me. He was carrying something from the back room. He set it down behind the counter and came around to meet me near the front door. "Your momma called a few minutes ago. She said to make sure you remember to pick up your dad's prescription."

I sighed and nodded. "Anything else?"

"Yeah, we have her prescription, too. Make sure you don't let her see you bring it in the house. She has a habit of accidently flushing them down the toilet. Your dad normally crushes one up in her orange juice in the morning."

He handed me the bag with my dad's bottle as well as the bottle of my mom's pills. I slipped Mom's medicine into my pocket.

"Is it helping?"

"I think so. When she manages to find them and get rid of them, she calls me a couple of times a day. When she's taking them… she's better."

"That's something at least," I said. Watching Mom go through this was hard at a distance. I can't imagine what Dad must be going through watching it day by day.

"I have your receipts here," Billy said. "I was going to mail them yesterday, but I figured if you were in, I might as well hand them to you."

"Thanks," I said as he handed them to me. I folded them up and put them in my shirt pocket.

"You're a good man, Dave," Sue said. "Not many sons would pay for their parents scripts the way you do."

"Well, not many pharmacists would work with me like this, so thanks to you and Billy as well."

"Not a problem. I have to admit, telling your folks their co-pay was five bucks a pop is pretty clever," Billy said. "I think your dad knows, though. He always grimaces whenever he gives me the money."

"I figure he does. But if we all pretend like it's not happening. I think he's happier."

Billy smiled and nodded. "It's good to see you, Dave. Give your mom a hug for me."

"Will do, Billy. Have a good day, Sue," I said as I left the store.

When I got in the car, I tossed the bag in the front seat and opened the glove compartment. Once I had stashed the receipts and mom's pills, I sat back up and immediately jumped in shock as a face was pressed up against my driver's side window.

Frank laughed as I opened the door.

"You are going to give me a heart attack one day," I said as I crawled out of the car. I was pissed, but was very happy to see my old friend.

"Sorry, man. Saw you getting in the car and when you looked away, I just had to," Frank said as he slapped me on the shoulder.

"Well, I'll let it slide this time," I said as I slapped him back. "What are you doing here? Don't you live in Wilcox now?"

"Yeah, but I run my drops all over the place. I'm about to head out to Cape for a delivery, but I should be back in the area tonight. Think you might want to head out to the Owl? Shoot some pool and down a few?"

"Not tonight, my folks will want to spend some time with me."

"Where's Lexi?" Frank asked as he looked in the car.

"She couldn't make it down this weekend, school stuff with Emma."

"Too bad, but that means we can hang out some tomorrow."

"Sure, swing by in the morning. I'm sure my dad will have something for us to do."

"It might be a little later. If you are going to be busy tonight, I'll probably hit a club in Cape and stay there," Frank said. "Do you remember Karen Sue? Her kid brother fronts a local band. He's playing at a club in town, and he's pretty good."

"Let me guess. You are staying with Karen tonight?"

Frank shrugged. "Sometimes I hang out with her when I head up to the Cape."

"So me bailing doesn't hurt your evening all that much?"

Frank laughed. "Aw, come on. I'd rather go drinking with you, but if you have to stay home, I'll call Karen and see what she is up to."

"Good luck."

"Thanks, and give your mom a hug for me."

Frank turned and walked over to his delivery truck.

I got back in my car and headed toward the house I grew up in. The trip across town was familiar and quick, although each time I drive through the old streets, I am surprised at what is and is not there. The old elementary school is there. I could probably walk in with my eyes closed and navigate the halls. But there is a new high school just a few blocks down. It's been there for fifteen years now, but it will always be the new high school to me.

The town has swelled and shrank in size since I left, but the new housing areas never reached the south end of town. The only house I lived in until I left for college sat on a wide plot with fallow farm fields behind it. The city limits were just on the other side of the Johnson's property next door, and past that were the heavy woods and hills which made up this part of the Mark Twain National Forest.

I noticed the soybeans on McKay's farm were starting to sprout as I pulled into my folk's driveway. There used to be three houses across the street from us, but old man McKay had bought them and cleared the land to expand his farm. Frank used to live in one of those houses and he was my best friend from as early as I could remember.

My car door had just swung open when I saw Dad turn the corner of the house. He was carrying a bag of trash out to the can.

"Davey," he called as I stepped out of the car. "Glad you made it."

"Me too, Dad," I said. "I'm looking forward to resting this weekend."

"A shame Lexi and Emma couldn't make it down, but school is school, I suppose."

I opened the back door to the car and pulled my bags out. I hadn't told them about Lexi wanting a trial separation. I had told Dad I was coming down to check on them, but I really did want to get away from the situation with Lexi for a few days as well.

"Now, about your mom," Dad said as he finished throwing the trash in the can. "She seems to think you are coming home from college. She says Diane will be by to see you tonight."

I sighed and shook my head. Diane was my mom's cousin. She had died of cancer twenty years before while I was still in college.

"So it's that bad, huh?"

"It's a bad day. They don't happen all that often when she keeps taking her meds, but they are getting more frequent."

"I picked up her prescription, they're in the glove compartment." The curtain at the front window moved as I was saying it.

"She's watching, I'm sure," Dad said. "I saw your eyes move to the front window. She knows there is something wrong, but she won't admit it. Don't bring it up if you don't want to be yelled at."

"Okay," I said. I reached in and grabbed the pharmacy bag from the front seat and started to open the glove compartment.

"Don't," Dad said. "Just bring mine in. We'll get hers later."

"She'll see?" I asked as I crawled out of the car.

"Yeah, if she thinks we slipped them in, she'll find them and throw them away."

I shook my head and picked up my bags. Dad shut the car door for me and we started walking toward the house.

"This way," Dad said as he headed to the garage.

He pressed the button to lift the door and led me in. He reached up on a high shelf and took down an old coffee can. He showed me the multiple medicine bottles that were in there.

"Six dollars worth of aspirin there, but it's better if she flushes those than her meds," he said with a wink. He took one of the bottles out and put the can back in its place.

"Here," he said as he slipped the bottle in my jacket pocket. "You'll see how good she is at this. She could have been a pickpocket in New York."

I laughed as Dad opened the door to the kitchen and led the way in.

"Guess who's here?" he asked.

"Who?" Mom responded, as if she hadn't been looking out the door.

"Hi Mom," I said as I stepped up from the garage. "Good to be home."

"David!" she said as she came over from the stove.

I saw the confusion in her eyes as she looked at me in genuine surprise.

"I…" She hesitated as she tried to make sense of it. "I'm so glad to see you. Did Lexi come?"

"No, Mom, she had to stay in Chicago. Emma had a school event this weekend."

"Emma. Yes, how is she?"

"She's doing well. She told me to give her grandma a kiss for her."

I kissed Mom on the cheek and saw Dad shaking his head. It must really be a bad day if she had forgotten her only grandchild.

"Well you take your bags to your room and I'll get dinner set. Diane…," she paused. "Diane would have been 68 this year. I'm sure she would have loved to have met Emma."

"She sure would have, Mom," I said. I carried my bags through the kitchen and down the short hallway to the room I grew up in. Dad had converted it to a guest room several years before, but it would always be my room.

I set my bags on the bed and felt at the pocket of my jacket. The bottle was gone. She must have slipped it out when she hugged me. No wonder Dad had to trick her into taking her meds.

I hung up my jacket and made a quick trip by the bathroom before I headed back to the kitchen. Mom was pulling a chicken out of the oven. She had stuffed it with her traditional sage stuffing and had a green bean casserole and a pan of sweet potatoes covered with marshmallows already on the table. A plate of sliced tomatoes sat on the counter. Mom always loved sliced tomatoes with any big holiday meal. I had seen the pumpkin pie cooling on the rack when I first came in. She really thought it was Thanksgiving. She was probably in a panic when she couldn't find the turkey and had made due with a whole chicken.

"Looks great, Mom."

"Thanks, David. I don't know what came over me this morning, I was just in the mood for a Thanksgiving-like meal."

"I don't know why we don't eat like this all the time," I said.

She smiled, but I could tell she was embarrassed. I hated to see her like that, knowing something was wrong but not being able to see it until the moment had passed. She was in a good state now.

Dad said grace as we sat around the table and caught up on news. The spring rains had come early and the fields looked good so far. Dad had planted a few tomatoes, but with his condition, he didn't think he could handle the full garden this year. Mom asked all sorts of questions about Emma and Lexi. It was hard not to bring up the problems, but I answered as much as I could.

The evening went by too quickly. I was glad I had told Frank I needed to spend time with my folks. As much as I had come down to help them any way they needed, they were helping me just as much. Just being away from the stress and pressure of my job, my marriage, my life was worth the eight hour drive and the extra vacation day. Tomorrow was Saturday and I would be able to help Dad with the repairs on his toolshed and could take them into Wilcox to stock up on any supplies they needed.

At eleven, they finally turned in. I thought about staying up and watching a ballgame from the west coast, but it had been a long day and I wanted to be fresh in the morning. I went and lay on the bed in my old room. The night was quiet. Not the quiet of silence, but the quiet of the country. The buzz of insects. The hoot of an owl in the woods. The distant cries of a coyote and the answering bark of dogs.

Sounds of my childhood comforted me as I slipped into sleep.

TWO

I sat up in a panic. My head felt like it had been dunked under rushing water and I felt as if I had been falling a great distance.

The room wasn't mine. Lexi wasn't next to me in the bed. I was at my parent's house. I took a deep breath as I recognized the room.

I closed my eyes and opened them again. I must have had a nightmare to have woken up that way. I looked around the room and wondered what time it was. There was enough ambient light outside to suggest it was morning, but the color of the light was wrong. The howls of the coyotes and dogs meant it was still late at night, but they were loud. And wrong.

I slipped out of bed as I heard movement in my parent's room across the hall.

"Davey?"

"I'm up, Dad. What's wrong?"

The door to my room opened and my dad stuck his head in.

"I don't know. Look outside."

I went to the window and lifted the curtain. Bright light poured in. Blue and green light. I squinted and looked up. The entire sky seemed to be on fire with shimmering sheets of light. Curtains of unnatural colors were visible in every direction.

"What is it?" I asked.

"Northern lights," Dad said. "Saw them occasionally when I was stationed in Maine with the Navy."

"Yeah," I said as I twisted my neck to look around the sky. "We get them every once in a while in Chicago. Have to usually drive out a bit to get a really good view. I didn't think they would get this far south."

"They don't," Dad said. "Never even seen a glimmer of them before. But I doubt they get this way even at the North Pole. Something is wrong."

I lowered the shade and looked at my dad. His voice had a strain to it, but this one was different than when he worried about mom, or worried about money. This was almost a scared sound.

"What do you mean?" I asked.

"Listen to those dogs," he said as he motioned outside. "Them and the coyotes aren't howling at each other right now. And all the birds are riled up, not just the owls."

I listened closely and could hear it. All of the local animals were upset.

"Let's turn on the TV and see what the news is reporting," I said. I started toward the living room.

"Power's out," Dad said. "No lights, no radio, no TV."

"Let's see if I can get a signal."

I went to the side table where I had left my phone. I had set it as an alarm clock, but the screen was off. I tried to turn it on, but it was dead.

"I charged this before I went to bed," I said.

"Your mom is looking for the flashlight in the kitchen," Dad said. "Although as bright as it is, don't think we really need it."

I sat down and grabbed my jeans from the floor. I had just zipped up when mom came in the room.

"I know these batteries are brand new," she said. "But it won't work."

"Go get some candles, then. We'll get some light," Dad told her.

I bent down and started putting on my shoes.

"Where are you going?" Dad asked.

"Out to the car, I can charge my phone out there. I can hit some news sites on the internet and find out what is happening."

I picked up the keys from the dresser and headed outside.

The night sky was so bright, I felt like I had stepped into a large auditorium. I could see the stars if I looked for them beyond the sheets of color that rippled across the sky. I stood in wonder for a few minutes and just stared at the brilliant show nature was treating us to.

"Hey," a voice behind me said. "Do you have a charger in your car?"

I turned and saw a teenage girl walking toward me.

"Uh, yeah. I do. I was about to charge my own phone on it. Who are you?"

"I'm Sarah," she said. She pointed behind her at the Johnson's house. "I'm staying with my grandparents this weekend."

"I'm David," I said. "This is my folk's house. Let me see if my charger will fit your phone."

We both had the same brand of phones so it looked like it would work.

"That was something, huh?" she said as I handed her phone back.

"What? The lights?"

"No, the flash. The lights were just there afterward."

"I was asleep, I guess. Were you awake?"

"Yeah, I was texting a friend. Phone died at the same time as the power went out. Freaky coincidence."

She was looking for confirmation, and she was scared.

"I guess. What happened?"

"Don't know. Just a big flash outside, lit up my whole room. I screamed and woke up Grams and Pop-pop. When I settled down, I realized the power was out and my phone was dead. That's when Felix went nuts and Grams had to let her out."

"Felix?"

"Their cat. Just started screaming and running everywhere. Guess the flash spooked her."

"I would imagine."

"What are those lights in the sky? Is it something the government is doing? It's kind of cool if so. Gives everybody enough light to see by if there is a power outage."

I shook my head. "No, those are the aurora borealis, the northern lights. The sky does that when the sun hits the atmosphere a certain way near the North Pole."

Sarah looked at me with a suspicious look.

"Are we near the North Pole? Isn't that in, like, near New York or something?" she asked.

I laughed. "No, the North Pole is quite a bit north of New York."

"Oh, well I'm from Louisiana so everything is north of us."

"Sarah!"

We both turned to see Rose Johnson calling to her granddaughter.

"I'm here, Grams," Sarah called. "This man is going to let me charge my phone."

Mrs. Johnson walked closer. "Is that David?"

"It is, Mrs. Johnson," I said. "How are you doing?"

"Well enough I suppose, what with being woken up in the middle of the night with all of this," she said looking up at the sky. "What are you doing out?"

"My phone died and I have a charger in my car."

Mrs. Johnson fished out a phone from her tattered robe.

"My phone died, too," she said. "Do you think you could charge mine?"

"Get in line, Grams," Sarah said. "I already asked him and he said he would do mine next."

I smiled and nodded. "Sure, if the charger will fit, I'll get everyone's up and going."

I walked toward the car as I hit the unlock button on my key fob. No click. I tried it again and there was the distinct lack of the sound of my doors unlocking. I tried the handle, but the door was locked. I shook my head and unlocked the door with my key.

"David, are you out here?" Mom called.

"He's out here, Abbey," Mrs. Johnson said. "He's going to help us charge our phones with his car."

"Be careful, David."

"I will, Mom," I said as I slid into the driver's seat. I wasn't sure what she thought charging a phone entailed, but I would be careful.

I fished out the phone charger from the glove compartment and slipped the bottle of mom's pills in my pocket since I saw them. I would just have to make sure I didn't walk close to the little pick-pocket when I went in the house.

I sat back up and jumped as Sarah had moved over to the car and was staring into the windshield with her face almost against the glass.

I thought about reaching over and squirting her with the windshield wiper fluid, but instead I just plugged in the charger and hooked my phone up.

"Did you find the charger?" Sarah asked.

"Yep," I said as I put the key in the ignition and started the car. Or at least I turned the key. The car didn't start. Didn't even try to turn over. I took the key out, looked at it, and tried again. Nothing.

"What's wrong?" Sarah asked.

"My car won't start," I said.

"So can you charge my phone?"

"Not if my car won't start."

"But, you said you could charge it." Her voice had the same whiny quality Emma's did when she was younger.

"How old are you, Sarah?" I asked.

"Fourteen. Why?"

"How long have you had a cell phone?"

"Since I was in first grade. My mom wanted a way for me to call her in case there was an emergency."

"I'm going to try my Dad's car and see if I can get my charger to work. If not, then you will have a story to tell your kids about how you were stuck without your phone for an entire night."

"Ha ha," she said. "I really want to take some pictures of the sky and send them to my friend Shelly."

I closed the door to my car and walked back to the house while laughing at the young girl. Emma was sixteen years old and would have likely made friends with Sarah. They were both bright but naïve girls who focused more on their friends than anything else. I was focused on the growing feeling something horrible had happened. But I wanted to see if my dad's car would start before I thought about it too much.

"Mom, where is Dad?"

"He's in the house. Why?"

"I just need to ask him something," I said as I left her talking with Mrs. Johnson.

I heard Sarah telling the older women how I wasn't going to be able to charge her phone as I entered the house. Mom had lit several candles, and the flickering light from their flames combined with the odd colored ribbons in the sky made the house seem more foreign to me than any time before.

"Dad?" I called as I moved through the house.

"In here, Davey," Dad replied.

I found him in the bathroom holding his electric razor.

"Shaving?"

He looked at me. "No, but I should be able to," he said.

He clicked the switch on and nothing happened.

"I leave this on the charger and shave with it every morning. Even with the power going out, I should be able to shave completely on the charge."

He placed the razor back on the charger. "Something odd is going on."

"I know," I said. "My phone died and so did Mrs. Johnson's and her granddaughter's. And my car won't start, won't even kick on."

"It's like all electricity just suddenly stopped." Dad had a very worried look on his face.

"Do you have anything that runs on 9-volts?" I asked.

"Not that I can think of. Why?"

"Just want to see something. What about your smoke detectors?"

Dad snapped his fingers. "Yes, they have 9-volts."

I walked out of the bathroom and looked down the hallway. I knew there was a smoke detector just outside my bedroom door. I reached up and could feel it.

"Here, stand on this." Dad had grabbed a small step stool from somewhere. I stepped up on it and pulled down the smoke detector. I quickly removed the battery and touched it to my tongue. The buzz and shock was there as the battery was live.

"Well," I said as I shook my head. "Batteries are still working. Let's see if your car will start."

We walked through the kitchen and into the garage. His large sedan was easy to move around as the ambient light shimmered in through the dirty windows set high on the garage wall.

Dad unlocked the driver's side door with his key and sat down.

"Here goes," he said as he turned the key in the ignition. Nothing. Not even the sputtery sounds that would have given me some hope.

"It's dead, Dad," I said.

"Yeah, she didn't even try to start up."

"Not the car, the world," I said. "Something horrible has happened and I don't know what it is, but nothing electrical seems to be working. Which doesn't make sense, because the battery was fine."

Dad closed the car door and came over to me.

"You know," he said as he squeezed my shoulder. "Back when I was in the Navy, they told us about all sorts of weapons that were being designed. One of those was something called an EMP bomb. Electric something or other."

"An electro-magnetic pulse," I said.

"Yeah, that sounds right. Anyway, they said if it was to go off, it would fry all the electrical systems but not hurt anyone. It was a way to knock out a city or a defensive position and take the people captive without having to kill them all."

"I don't know if that is what happened, though. Look at the sky. It doesn't look like it was a local event."

"Maybe, maybe not. But not much we can do about it tonight. Let's see if we can get some news tomorrow."

"Sounds like a plan. Wish I could call Lexi and Emma and make sure they are alright."

"I'm sure they are. They are probably asleep and will see the news tomorrow and try to get ahold of you."

I nodded. "You're right, we should get whatever sleep we can. The animals are still freaking out. Don't know how I will sleep with all of that racket."

Dad laughed. "You live in Chicago! When we visited, I couldn't believe how loud it was at night. I didn't think I could ever get to sleep."

"I live in Oak Park, Dad. The city itself is much noisier."

He shook his head and held up his hands. "If you say so, but I constantly heard cars and trucks on the highway. Out here are only the sounds nature provides."

"Nature is providing plenty of light and sound tonight," I said. "But I bet I can get back to sleep."

"I'm normally up about five. What time do you think it is?"

I shrugged. "Don't know. Sarah said it was about three. She was texting on her phone with some friends when it happened."

"Sarah?"

"The Johnson's granddaughter."

"Oh, yeah. I've seen her around a few times. Three is early even for me. I'll go get your mom and we'll try to get some sleep."

"Night, Dad."

I went back to my room and shut the door. I kicked off my shoes and shrugged out of my jeans. I lay on the bed and tried to sleep, but the room was too bright.

I was worried about Lexi and Emma. Is what happened affecting them? If so, would they be completely freaked out? Or would they sit tight and wait for news? I thought Lexi would be able to handle it, but she had changed so much in the last few years. It wasn't like I was living with a stranger, but she had changed. We all changed over time. We grew wiser and more set in our ways, more mellow and more short tempered, all the contradictory changes that move us from adolescence into adulthood and towards old age.

But she had changed dramatically in the last few years. She had lost the joy and sparkle in her eye when I would walk in the room. She found ways to spend time alone when she could. I wanted to talk with her about it, but I always felt as if it would crumble apart in my hands if I tried to take hold of it. So I watched it slowly disintegrate.

Wilson Harp   EMP

That was the path I was on. I wished someone or something could show me how to stop it from falling apart.

With all of the fear over the events of the night, it was still my personal problems that meandered through my mind as I lay in my old bedroom. Somehow, I managed to fall asleep.

THREE

The next morning wore the appearance of normality. The smell of bacon and coffee told me Mom had cooked breakfast while I slept. I headed to the bathroom to relieve myself and then brush my teeth.

"Morning, Davey," Dad said as I approached the bathroom. "Toilet isn't flushing right and the sink has almost no pressure."

I turned the cold water on in the sink and the water dribbled out. I brushed my teeth and then used the bathroom. The flush was fine, but barely a trickle of water filled the tank again. After a few seconds I realized the main water tank in Kenton was probably empty from the town all participating in their daily morning rituals and the pump that forced the water up was probably off line. I decided even trying for a shower was a useless endeavor and headed to the kitchen for breakfast.

"Morning, dear," Mom said as she saw me sit at the table. "How do you want your eggs?"

"Scrambled will be fine, Mom," I said as I looked at the hearty breakfast she had laid out on the table. Bacon, biscuits and gravy, fried potatoes and a cut up cantaloupe made my normal breakfast of a bowl of oatmeal and coffee seem sparse. A cup of coffee and a large glass of orange juice stood ready at my place at the table.

"I think I'm going to walk into town and find out some information," I told Dad.

He was looking through some old papers he had pulled out of a dirty manila folder.

"Sounds like a good idea, Davey. But I may need you before it gets dark tonight," he said.

Mom came and took my plate to serve the eggs as I looked closer at the papers Dad held.

"Is that the land deeds for the house?" I asked.

"Yes, and for the Anderson's old place as well," he said. "Looking for where their pump was in relation to our house."

"Pump? I don't remember them ever having a pump."

"They had it sealed up when they got city water. It was a few years before you were born. I helped Charlie cap the well. I still have the old pump itself in the shed."

I remembered seeing an old pump in Dad's shed when I was growing up, but I never thought to ask where it came from.

"If we need to access that well, we will have to dig into the soybean field," I said.

"Why on earth would we need to access a well?" Mom asked as she sat my plate in front of me. "The water will be back on a little later. Just like the power."

"I'm sure you are right, dear," Dad said as he flashed her a big smile. "Just part of my silliness, I suppose."

"Well don't drag David into your silliness. He is too old and smart to start thinking that way."

I smiled as I ate my breakfast. It felt like home with Mom and Dad bickering over little things. I realized anything they disagreed about over breakfast was not serious. They never picked at each other about things that couldn't be changed or were in any way permanent. It was about things that would easily be forgotten within a few hours at the most.

It made me wonder about how I spoke to Lexi. Did I disrupt our time together with issues that stressed her out? Did I question her about things she had no control over?

"David?" Mom asked.

"What?"

"I asked you when you were planning on going into town."

"Oh. Sorry, got lost in thought there. I'm heading in right after breakfast."

"Could you swing by and check on Ruth Walters? She lives alone now and I don't know if anyone will think to check on her with the power out."

I looked at my plate and was shocked that all of my breakfast had been eaten.

"Yeah, Mom. No problem. Give me her address and I'll check on her."

Mom went to look for a paper and pen. When she left the room, my Dad leaned over.

"Did you bring her pills in, last night?"

"Yeah," I whispered back. "I put them in the second drawer of my dresser."

"Ok," he said. "I'll go look for them. I won't find any magazines in there, will I?"

"No," I said as I stood. "That was over twenty years ago. Let it go."

He smiled and went back to looking at the papers in the folder.

I went over to refill my coffee cup, but the pot was empty.

"I'm sorry, David," Mom said as she came back in the kitchen. "There is something wrong with the water, so I just used a bottled water to fill the coffee maker. Just enough for a small cup for each of us this morning."

"I better get going," I said as I put my cup down in the sink. "I'll be back by dinner time."

"Take a notepad and a pen," Mom said as she handed me a slip of paper with her friend's address on it. "You never know if you will need to leave a note with someone."

It was sound advice, so I looked in the utility drawer and grabbed a pen. I picked up a small notepad on the kitchen counter next to the phone, scribbled on it to make sure the pen worked and placed them both in my shirt pocket. I went to my room and put on my shoes and picked up my wallet and keys from the dresser.

"Be safe, David. And stop by the pharmacy if you can. Maybe he has the prescriptions ready," Dad said as I left the house.

I nodded as I said goodbye. I knew what Dad was thinking. Even though they had just had their prescriptions filled, it wouldn't hurt to have an extra month on hand. I'm sure he already has a spare bottle somewhere in the house, but I knew he was as worried as I that this outage would be longer than a day or two.

It was only about three miles from the house to where the five and dime on Vinson Street used to be. Frank and I would make the trip each Saturday. Sometimes we would buy packs of baseball cards and open them to see who we got. Other times we would buy some candy and split a soda. I realized even though I was older the road into town now seemed longer and more menacing. Of course I was on foot now, and back then Frank and I lived on our bikes.

The number of houses were fewer. The McKay's had bought all of the land on the west side of the highway for their soybeans. On the east side, some of the houses I remember riding past had been torn down as well. In a few cases, new houses sat where others had been, but some lots were barren. I remember there had been some bad flooding over the years, and some of those houses had been total losses.

"Hello."

A faint voice caught my ear and I turned to look. A frail looking woman stood in the doorway of a dingy house. The early April growth of weeds seemed to be reinforcing the wild lawn left from the autumn before.

"Hello," I said with a wave. I turned off the shoulder of the highway and walked onto her driveway.

"Are you heading into town?" She asked.

"I am, ma'am."

"Can you ask them if they can check on my water and electricity? My grandson said he paid them last month, but I think they cut it off anyway last night."

"I'll ask, ma'am. But there is a power outage, I am afraid. My folk's house lost power last night as well, and they must be having problems with the water tower as well."

"Oh. Well thank you. You look familiar. Do I know you?"

"I'm not sure. I'm David Hartsman. My folks live over there. When I was a kid, this was Allen Stewart's house."

"David Hartsman! I'll be. Allen is my grandson. I'm his grandma, Jana. I remember you now."

"It's good to see you again, Mrs. Stewart."

"No, I'm his momma's mother. I'm Mrs. Grant."

"I'm going into town, now Mrs. Grant. I'll stop by and let you know what is going on when I come back later this afternoon."

"Thank you, David. I'll let you get on your way."

I continued on toward town as I tried to remember what I could of Allen. His dad had left the family before Allen went to grade school. He was a few years younger than me and Frank, and at the time we didn't want a younger kid hanging around with us. From what I recalled, his mother had a reputation for sleeping around town and she was constantly in trouble with the law. She liked booze and pot. Even the kids in high school learned to stay away from her as she was always caught up in one mess after another.

I think I remember Allen talking about his grandmother coming to live with them. At the time I guess I thought his grandmother must have needed help because she was old, but now I realize she probably came to help take care of Allen because his mom was such a mess.

As I crossed Miller Road, the fields to my left turned into a subdivision that would not have been out of place forty miles outside Chicago. The housing was more tightly packed together than the town I grew up in, and yet somehow the intervening years had made this style of suburban living feel more like home to me. There were several other people, none of whom I recognized, walking toward town along the highway ahead of me a ways. It looked like they were walking as a group and I wondered if there weren't people already talking about what happened and making plans on how to cope.

My legs were starting to burn as I moved past the old fire station. It was some sort of artist shop now. I stopped and rested against the brick wall. A huge mural of flowers and rainbows dominated the side of the crumbling building. This fire station used to be just inside the actual town's borders. Kenton had expanded far enough south to put my folks inside the town by the time I had graduated high school, but if it shrank back to the old fire station, I don't think anyone would notice.

I wondered what time it was and my hand instinctively went to my front pocket for my phone. When I realized what I had done, I shook my head and looked up to the sky. The sun was out and about halfway from the horizon to the noon position. Since it was early April, I figured it must be between nine thirty and ten in the morning. Maybe a little later, but not much.

A couple rode by me on bikes as I pushed myself away from the wall and on into town. I would have to see if my old bike was still in the garage somewhere, that was certain. As I left the fire station, I was glad to see the sidewalk. I had never really noticed the lack of sidewalks along the highway before. At least there were no cars I had to keep watch for. Of course, if my car had worked, I would have driven it into town.

Soon there were groups of people along my path. The first was a group of three young women. They all looked very upset and each held cell phones in their hands. The snippets of conversation I grabbed as I passed by all seemed to be focused on what they would do to whoever was responsible for their lack of cell service.

The further I walked, the more groups there were. Most just laughed and talked as if they hadn't seen each other in some time. Perhaps that was the case. How many of my friends in Chicago had I communicated with several times a day and yet not actually seen in months? If the situation was not so severe, I might have thought a few days of no smartphones and laptops would have a refreshing effect on many relationships.

But what happened in the night was severe. I knew it was, as did others, from the comments I heard as I walked by. While those around them chatted and talked about the odd occurrence, those who seemed to know had a haunted look in their eyes. When they saw me, there was a slight nod or wince. After I had passed several larger groups, I noticed a small tail of followers.

I wanted to tell them I had no idea where I was going, but I kept walking. I knew I would recognize what I was looking for when I saw it.

I pulled the slip of paper Mom had given me out of my shirt pocket and read the address. It wasn't far from where I was, but I knew I needed information first.

"There," a man behind me said. He was pointing up the street. I hesitated and a few of the men who had followed me to that point walked forward instead. Now, I followed them. A few men stood near an old streetlight in front of the library along the far edge of the town square. Most were older and one wore a policeman's uniform.

"Carl, you need to let them know what is happening," one of the men said loudly as I approached.

"How?" the one name Carl asked. "How am I supposed to let anyone know what is happening when I have no idea."

"You can at least tell them we don't know when the power will be back on," another man said.

"Even if I could somehow piece it together, how am I supposed to tell everybody?"

"What about your bullhorn?" one of the men asked. "You have that in your office, don't you? You use it when we have the fair every year."

"If it's like everything else, it won't work," the man in the police uniform said.

"Thank you, Gary," Carl said. "The problem we are facing is none of us knows what is going on and we can't get in touch with anyone who does."

"I know what's going on," a booming voice said.

I turned and looked over to the steps of the library. There was a tall man in a red t-shirt and blue jeans. He had wild bushy hair and a long beard. He also had a rifle slung over his shoulder and a canteen hanging from his belt.

"Who are you?" Carl asked.

"That is Ted Riggins," Gary said. His hand slipped down to his belt and rested easily on his sidearm.

"Morning Deputy," Ted said. "And the answer to your question, Mayor, is that we experienced a massive EMP last night."

I was shocked at the conviction he said this with.

"What is an EMP?" someone asked.

"The sun let loose with a giant solar flare," Ted said. "It traveled straight at us and hit the magnetic field around the earth. It was like a giant planet sized bolt of lightning hit us dead on."

The murmurs and questions started growing louder. I glanced around and noticed more and more people drifted toward the crowd.

"Hold on," Ted said. He yelled to be heard over the crowd. When the volume shifted down, he spoke again.

"The power is gone, at least from this area. Almost every electric device is fried out. That means the transformers which allow electricity to flow through the power lines, the switch boxes which control the communications, and even the pump that keeps the water supply going."

"What do we do?" a woman asked.

"First, we don't panic," Ted said. "We don't know how widespread the EMP was so we might be contacted in a few days from those who are in charge of an emergency like this. In the meantime, we need to have some volunteers who can help communicate what needs to be done."

The crowd pushed forward with questions and calls drowning out Ted's voice.

Carl, the mayor of Kenton, worked his way up to the unkempt Ted Riggins. They spoke for a few seconds and the mayor motioned people to silence.

"We need thirty volunteers," he said. "There are around thirty-five hundred people in and around Kenton and each volunteer will have about a hundred people to get information to. If you are willing, go stand next to the wall." He pointed to the wall along the side of the post office.

I found myself over by the wall along with most of those who had followed me toward the town square. I glanced around and realized while there were a few women who had moved over to the wall, most were men in their thirties and forties. Family men, I figured by their looks. Men, like me, who had the responsibility of others to consider. And yet we were all volunteering to help this shaggy man, who the policeman was concerned about, spread information that would keep people calm.

A man bumped into me and apologized. I looked over to tell him it was alright, but instead I stared in amazement. It was Kenny Dawson. I had not seen him since he graduated high school. He was one of the few black kids to go to our district.

"Kenny," I said. "Man, look at you."

"I'm sorry," he said. "I'm bad with names."

"David Hartsman. You graduated when I was a freshman."

I could see he still had no idea who I was.

"It's alright, Kenny. You were older and I was just a freshman when you left."

"Sorry, man," he said. "I just… there's a lot I don't like to remember from back then, you know?"

"Yeah, I'm sure."

When he said that, I remembered his family's house burned down one Christmas day. The fire inspector said it was arson, but no one was ever charged. I also remembered he and his sister had to deal with the racist attitudes of many in school.

"We have more than enough, it seems," the mayor said as he walked over to the volunteers. "Let's go into the meeting room and sort this out."

A pudgy man with a shock of white hair nodded and unlocked the front doors to the library.

"If you are a volunteer, follow us in. If not, please go home and wait for further information," the mayor said to the crowd gathered in the square. Except for the volunteers who filed into the library, no one else moved from where they were.

The meeting room in the library was just as I remembered it. The town council met there and the committee for the Thanksgiving parade used it as a planning room. My mother had been part of that committee for as long as I could remember. As a kid, I would grab a Hardy Boys book and read it while they had their meetings.

I took a seat near the window and Kenny sat next to me. Ted walked over to Kenny and said something. It was too low for me to hear, but Kenny smiled at Ted and motioned toward me.

"What was that?" I asked.

"He just wanted to know if I knew anyone here. I told him we went to high school together."

I smiled at Kenny and nodded. A gavel struck the podium and the few people who had not sat down found seats.

"Ladies and gentlemen," the mayor began. "I don't recognize several of you, so let me begin by introducing myself. I am Carl Mueller and I am the mayor here in Kenton. I want to introduce you to—"

"Hold it," Ted said suddenly. "I mean no offense, Mayor. But, we need to get moving."

Carl nodded and sat down in a chair behind the podium. Ted walked to the front and pointed out the windows.

"As of now, we are living in a different world. In a few days, maybe we will be back to our old world, but the decisions we make in the next few hours will set our course if this problem lasts for weeks, months, or years."

Murmurs picked up and Ted had to pause for a few seconds. The mayor stood up and pounded the podium with his gavel and then handed it to Ted when the room quieted again.

"How many here rode bikes into town?" Ted asked.

About six hands went up.

"Good, you will be our messengers for today," the bristly man continued. "We will need to go into every garage and shed and look for bicycles tomorrow. We need to be able to stay mobile and spread out a bit. If we all gather into town, we will run into problems."

"What kinds of problems?" a man in a John Deere cap asked.

"Health issues if this goes on too long. So we need bikes, skateboards, inline skates, and anything else that will work as well."

"Horses?" Kenny asked.

He was looking out the window. A woman was riding up to the town square on the back of a horse. My breath caught in my throat as I recognized her. Anne Franklin had just ridden back into my life.

FOUR

I stood and hurried out the front of the library. Anne was dismounting when I stopped at the top of the steps and just stared at her. I didn't know what to say or if she would even recognize me. It had been nineteen years since we had last spoken face to face and I was as nervous as I was the first time I had spoken to her six years before that.

She finished hitching her horse's reins to a park bench and started up the stairs. She stopped as her eyes slipped across my face and recognition flared up.

"David, how good to see you," she said with a bright smile. "In Kenton for a quick visit?"

I stammered for a second as I tried to get my bearings. We hadn't parted on good terms, and yet she spoke like it had been just months or even days since we last spoke. The oddest part was it felt normal and natural.

"Yes," I said. "Got here last night. Just in town to check up on Mom and Dad."

"And how are they?" Anne asked as she looked around the town square.

"They're good. Mom is… doing okay I guess, and Dad is still kicking along."

"What's going on in there?" she asked as she looked at the library doors.

"The mayor called for volunteers to help spread information on what we need to do."

"Mueller knows what's going on?"

"No. A guy named Ted something or other."

"Ted Riggins?"

"Yeah, that sounds right."

"Huh," she said with a surprised inflection.

"You know him?"

"A bit. He buys supplies from me occasionally. Not a great rider, but he takes care of his horses pretty well."

"He seems to think it was an EMP from the solar flare last night."

"A what?"

"An electro-magnetic pulse. Dad thought the same."

"Let's get in there and see what he has to say," she said.

I followed her into the meeting room where we slipped in to stand in the back. Ted had a list of items written on a movable whiteboard behind him. I pulled out the small notebook and pen Mom had pushed on me before leaving the house and jotted down the items: water, medicine, food, contact.

"The pharmacy will be locked down when we leave this meeting," Ted was saying. "We will attempt to make sure everyone gets the medicine they need, but after two weeks we will likely start seeing shortages. When you contact the houses in your area, check to see if there are any doctors, nurses or anyone with E.M.T. training. We will also need any medical books we can acquire."

People were jotting notes on whatever paper they seemed to have scrounged up. I leaned against the wall and listened as I wrote what I needed to remember.

"We will need to meet here again tomorrow to send more information out," Ted said. "If you cannot make it back, we need to know now. I would like to have at least six runners who can get information quickly to the different volunteers. If possible, we will set up an alarm system."

Several people shifted and muttered as he talked.

"Shouldn't we bring everyone into town?" one man asked.

"No," Ted answered. "If we are only going to be out of power for a few days, there is no need. If we are going to be out of power for more than a couple of weeks, we will want people as spread out as possible to prevent any spread of disease."

"What kind of disease are we talking about?" Mayor Mueller asked.

"Mostly waterborne. Cholera, for example. That's why we need to make sure we have fresh water to drink. Any water anyone may get from their pipes should be boiled. If we can reopen a few of the wells around the area, that would be great. I have a couple of hand pumps at my house and if we check the area, we might find some hidden away in old garages."

I raised my hand. "My father has one and was looking for the Anderson's old pump location when I left the house this morning."

"Good," Ted said. "Who are you and where is the well located?"

"I'm David Hartsman and my folks live at the south edge of town on Granger."

"Good. Looks like you know Anne, and she has a horse today. I'm going to let you and Anne contact everyone south of Miller and west of Granger with the information we need to get out. Anne, you can let everyone know along Balsam Road when you head back home."

Ted explained what the priorities were, to keep everyone safe and calm. The pharmacy would be secured and all the other stores shut for a few days. The volunteers were to take notes on each house and get names and ages of everyone who lived in each residence. He said it was important to have an accurate census since there might be people in the area who didn't normally live there, and some who lived in the area might be away.

I thought of Frank and how he was likely trapped over in Cape Girardeau. It was about two hours away by car, but still over a hundred miles on foot. The four miles to the library seemed like a long walk, I could only imagine if Frank tried to walk back to Wilcox.

Ted went on to say folks should keep their freezers shut for the next couple of days and eat as much food from their refrigerators as possible. Then, work on cooking and keeping everything in the freezer. Canned goods should be saved and anything that could sit in the pantry should be eaten after food from the freezer was gone.

I wasn't sure how long Ted thought this outage might continue, but I suspected the people of Kenton would eat better than normal for the next several days before facing any real trauma of low food supplies.

We were told to check with any families with children to make sure they had adequate food. Children would be the first hit with dehydration and malnutrition, and with many families probably having more food in their refrigerators or freezers than they could finish in a few days, it made no sense to have some children go hungry before food in town had a chance to spoil.

When Ted first started speaking, the mayor and the deputy seemed ill at ease. Their confusion and uncertainty of the situation seemed to let Ted take the reins even though doubts were evident. But as he spoke, I saw the look of confidence grow on the faces of Mayor Mueller and the lawman. Ted spoke as a man who had prepared for this day, and from the comments I heard, he likely had. He understood the limitations we faced, he knew what needed to be prioritized, and he even described the emotional state we were laboring under.

"What you are feeling," he said, "is called 'normalcy bias.' It means the situation is so far beyond what you can consider normal, you are just rejecting it as reality. The facts, ladies and gentlemen, are this: we have no water, no food, no power, no transportation, and no help on the way. Every drop of water, every morsel of food, and every bit of help will come from the people in this room and how they react and respond to the reality we face."

Thoughtful expressions turned panicked as those who listened really let the situation sink in. The knot that had been sitting deep in my gut ripped open as I realized what he was saying. My God! Lexi and Emma were in Chicago and I had no way of reaching them or even knowing if they were okay.

"David," Anne said. She was bent over, helping to keep me upright. My knees had buckled and I discovered I was kneeling on the floor.

Ted had stopped speaking and just looked at the crowd. A wave of comprehension had swept across the room and there were more than a few people who had collapsed like I did.

"What do we do, Riggins?" Deputy Gary asked after a few seconds.

"We make a plan and we stick to it. When people start realizing what we are facing, they will need a plan to lean on."

"Why are you asking him?" a woman exclaimed.

"Yeah," a man added. "Who put him in charge?"

"He's been talking about the end of the world for years," another man said. "How do we know he didn't have something to do with it!"

Kenny walked to the front and turned to address the room.

"I was in New Orleans when Katrina hit," he said. "I was waiting on help after the storm, but help never came. I eventually walked out and found a group of people who got me to Shreveport. I thought maybe I could get help there, but there was no help. I didn't have any kids and I didn't have any family nearby. So, I caught a ride up to Memphis and then made my way back to Kenton."

A few of the gathered men and women nodded as Kenny spoke. They had heard the story it seemed. Most of the others fidgeted and looked uncomfortable.

"I guess my point is, we can't rely on anyone else. Especially not the government," said Kenny. "We tried that in New Orleans when we should have been prepared and should have taken care of ourselves and each other. I would love nothing more than to see a car pull into Kenton with a group of men who will tell us where to go to make sure we have plenty of food and water, but after what happened in the sky last night, I don't think that is in the cards. Do you?"

The room became silent. The sky was lit up from one side of the horizon to the other. Thousands of miles of sky all energized by something.

Mayor Mueller stepped forward and looked at Kenny and Ted. He turned back to face the volunteers. "These men are right. We have to be our own rescuers. If there is no objection, I am going to put Ted Riggins in charge of the relief effort officially."

Nods and voiced affirmations greeted the announcement. Something as simple as the man elected to be in charge making a decision seemed to calm the nerves of everyone in the room.

"Thank you, Mayor," Ted said as he pointed back at the white board. "I think we have everything we need today. We can meet again tomorrow morning and start figuring out what we have available and what we need. Remember to write down the situation of anyone who needs specific help."

Anne let go of my arm I didn't realize she was still holding.

"I guess we need to get going and start telling people what is going on," she said.

"Yeah. But first, I promised my mom I would check on a friend of hers." I held up the piece of paper with the address.

"Who does she want you to check on?"

"Ruth Walters."

Anne sighed. "Ruth lives out in Gainesboro now. Her daughter set her up in the nursing home."

"How long ago?"

"Maybe three years."

I nodded and slipped the note back in my shirt pocket.

Anne smiled at me. There were a few tears in her eyes.

"I lost my mom the same way," she said. "If you need anything, I'm here for you."

We walked out of the library as the mayor, the deputy, Kenny and Ted talked near the white board. Besides us, all the others had left.

"I heard you had moved back to town," I said.

"Well nothing's wrong with your memory, you must have heard that ten years ago," she said.

"Has it been that long?"

She nodded. "Yeah. When Dad died, I quit my job in Denver and moved back here to help Mom."

"You kept the stables going?"

"No. I still do taxes, just out of my house now instead of working for a big company. Mom decided having a bunch of horses was too much work. Bonnie and Clyde are enough now."

"I'm sorry I didn't come back for your folks funerals," I said.

She laughed. It was a sound that pulled me back almost thirty years.

"David, if you had come to my dad's funeral, he would have climbed out of that casket and tried to kill you."

"Probably," I said as a sheepish smile crept up my face. "But I should have come back for your mom, at least."

"That is true," Anne said. "Mom always liked you."

I thought about just walking away, like I had thirty years before. This time I had nothing to gain by staying. Nothing but an old friend, anyway.

"I guess we better mount up. Are you riding in front?" I asked.

"Maybe. Are you a better rider than you were in high school?"

"Hey," I whined with mock indignation. "I was a good rider."

"No," Anne said with a laugh. "You weren't. And I can't imagine you have gotten any better living in the big city."

We walked over to the bike rack where she had tethered her horse. The crowd outside the library had started to thin out. Little clumps of people dotted the area, either catching up with neighbors and laughing, or listening intently to one of the volunteers that had been tasked with preparing the town for what was to come.

"Hey Bonnie," Anne said as she untied the mare's reins. "This is my friend David and we are both going to need a ride, okay?"

Bonnie seemed very calm as I approached her. I reached out to stroke her nose and she looked at me as if taking measure of my ability.

"Don't worry, girl. He'll be riding behind me," Anne said as if she could read my mind.

Anne swung up into the saddle like a star from a 60's western. A smooth, single motion that looked so simple and effortless. She held her hand out for me and I exhaled a breath I didn't realize I had been holding. I just didn't want to fall on my face like I had so many years ago when I visited her house for the first time.

She slid her foot from out of the stirrup as I stepped up to start my first attempt at riding a horse in close to thirty years. I grabbed her wrist tightly and she pulled up on my arm and helped me get the momentum needed to swing into the saddle. I was surprised as I felt myself settle into the right position.

"Not bad, David. At least you remember how to get in the saddle."

"As long as you don't give her the bit, I should be able to stay put," I said as I rested my hands on Anne's hips.

Our conversation was casual as we road south out of town. With each minute and each sentence, the awkwardness of our past and the tension of the present situation seemed to melt away.

We stopped and gave basic information to several small knots of people who had gathered at some of the crossroads. Each group seemed mollified as we explained what we knew, what we did not know, and how the committee had decided to spread news of what we as a town would do to get through this bizarre and mysterious time.

We made the turn west on Miller Road and I hopped off and started going house to house on foot. Anne rode on to the end of the development and we met in the middle some hours later. We then headed back to Granger and took turns with the houses on the way south.

The sun was sliding down the western sky when I spotted my folks house. There was a small crowd gathered on the front lawn just past where my car was parked. It looked like the crowd was composed almost entirely of grey haired men.

One of the gathered men pointed toward the horse and pair of riders. The crowed quieted and waited. Calls of greetings to Anne started as we came closer, and by the time I slid out of the saddle, smiles and casual chatter was wide spread.

"Davey," my dad said. He left the crowd and walked to the horse.

He looked tired and worn. I could tell by his clothes he had been working in the dirt all day.

"Dad," I said. "How is everything here?"

I looked closer and most of the men were in the same condition as my dad. They looked dirty and tired, but they all had big smiles,

"Good, good. We were able to get three wells reopened today and we think we know where another four are."

"That's fantastic," Anne said. "How did you get that much of a jump on the rest of us?"

Dad shrugged and looked around at the assembled men. "I guess we are from a generation that doesn't need to be told what to do. We figured if there was no water from the town, we would go back to the way many of us got water as kids. We went back to the well."

"Good job, Dad," I said. "Anne, do you want to have dinner with us tonight."

"No," Anne said. She was shading her eyes as she looked to the west. "We need to hit the rest of the houses on Granger, and then I need to get the houses along Balsam. Plus, I need to get back to my place and take care of the animals. But I'll be here early tomorrow morning with Clyde. You can ride him if you want."

"Sounds good," I said. "You have a good night and don't stay up too late."

Anne's laugh always reminded me of rain on a sheet of crystal in the past. Light and playful. It surprised me to hear a throaty, deep chuckle come from her. A type of laugh her father always had.

She waved and let Bonnie canter south along the road. After the Johnson's, there was no homes for a full mile. At the bridge over Carter's Creek, the last people that could said to be part of Kenton, lived in small collection of old houses and mobile homes in a large wooded area right off Granger. Once Anne let them know what Ted had said, she would ride back up to Miller and then west toward Balsam. I could only imagine how sore she would be tomorrow.

"Be careful, Davey," Dad said as we turned towards the house.

"How do you mean?"

"You may be having a tough time with Lexi, but you need to mend those fences, not go looking to the past."

I didn't think it was any of his business, and I wasn't considering getting together with Anne, but I didn't want to discuss it with a crowd of men around us.

"What's the word, Pat? Your boy bring any news back?"

Dad motioned to me and I realized I was expected to report information and instructions to men I would have been intimidated to address by their first names just twenty years ago. It had been that many years since I had seen most of them.

"Ted Riggins has been appointed the head of the effort to get us through this," I said. Several of the men nodded and a fair number frowned at this first bit of information. Most remained impassive as if the name did not mean anything to them. It probably didn't.

"He is of the opinion a massive solar flare created an electro-magnetic pulse that has disabled the electrical power for at least this part of the country."

Murmurs started and several men started to ask questions.

"Quiet!" Dad said. He didn't yell, but his voice took on the sharp report of a cracking bullwhip.

"The first thing Riggins said we should do is make sure we have plenty of water. Looks like the men here have already been working on that, so at least the south part of town is ahead of the game by a day."

The men smiled at this and several clapped each other on the back.

"We don't know when, or if, we will get any news from the government about what is happening or when it will be fixed. So, the first things we need to do is keep the freezers closed, not open packaged or canned food, and cook and eat everything in our refrigerators."

"Let's get a fire going!" someone said. I thought it was Luke Carter, a man of large appetites and larger talk. Several others cheered at his proclamation.

"That's a good idea," Dad said. "The rest we can talk about tomorrow. We have a little daylight left, so let's get a large cooking area setup and everyone can gather and eat together."

"We don't need to go through that trouble, do we?" I asked. "Most everyone out here has propane stoves, they should still work."

"We need the wood ash, Davey," Dad said. "We need to get as much wood ash as we can gather. Having a large fire pit will help gather it, and people can cook and have a sense of being together."

"Why do we need wood ash?"

"Tomorrow when we build our outhouse, you'll see why."

"Outhouse?"

"No water pressure, remember?"

I hadn't really thought about it. I did need to pee, but the need hadn't been at the level of discomfort where I sought out a place to relieve myself.

"Where have you been going?" I asked.

"Behind the garage," he said.

"And Mom?"

Dad sighed and looked down. "I'm not proud, Davey. I slipped some strong sleeping pills into your mom's coffee. She's been asleep most of the day. I had Rose come over and keep an eye on her. I just didn't think she would be capable of dealing with all the changes today brought."

I nodded and put my hand on his shoulder. As hard as it was for me to deal with her decline from a distance, it paled in comparison to the pain he must go through daily.

"I'll go check out the back of the house," I said. "You see about getting your buddies organized for a neighborhood cookout."

FIVE

The cookout that night was one to remember. Almost a hundred people, from close to sixty houses, came with whatever food they had in their refrigerators to cook and eat. Six tables were set up to hold all of the food, and most people either sat on blankets or stood and watched the sky as the sun set.

The northern lights were almost as bright as they had been the night before. Long after it should have been dark, there was still plenty of light for the children to run and play. The adults tended to either stand in small groups or move from small group to small group. Those that roamed were trying to gather information. Most was innocuous, but I heard several ask questions that made me uncomfortable. One man, in particular, was very interested in whether people thought they should be hunting and what kinds of guns they had.

I pulled my dad to the side and asked about that man.

"Brent Talley. Keep an eye on him," Dad said. "Sounds like he is wanting to know who is armed and who isn't. I understand he spent some time in prison for armed robbery. There are always those who will take advantage of a situation however they can."

I nodded and went back to watching the crowd. Luke Carter was another one of those making the rounds of the small groups, but instead of gathering information, he was letting everyone know what was going to happen in the next couple of days. He had a genial manner as he talked to each group, and I noticed the subtle way he changed his tone and wording as he started speaking.

To small groups of men, he smiled and talked about how glad they would be when the power came back on because they were going to have to dig and carry all sorts of things for the next few days. To groups with women or young children, he dropped his tone and looked wistful as he wondered what would happen if it lasted more than a day or two. He waited for them to get a little concerned at his questions and then reassured them it would be okay.

He was preparing people, and he wasn't scaring them. He was just letting them know it would get tougher, but we, as a community, would find our way out of this tough spot.

I had to get him together with Ted. If Luke Carter could take the instruction and information and spread it in the way he was working this impromptu cookout, then we may not face any panicked people at all.

After eating a few bites, I realized I was very hungry. I had not eaten since breakfast and it had been a long day. I felt guilty eating food others had brought, especially considering how little food there might be in the future, but everyone encouraged me to try a bit of everything. None of the food would be good past morning, anyway. There was no way to keep it.

So I ate. Food Lexi would have forbidden me was piled onto my plate. I knew I might be sick in the morning, but I kept eating.

As I sat in the grass and looked around, I could see many of the children headed back to their parents. Toddlers and babies were already asleep, and those that were shy of their teen years were staying awake through sheer willpower. Most of the adults were yawning and looking up at the unnaturally bright sky.

"Come on, Davey."

I turned to see Dad motion me to the house. Mom stood in the doorway. She stared at the sky in wonder.

I stood and was surprised to see Luke Carter head toward the front door as well.

When I entered the house, Luke was sitting at the dining room table along with my parents.

"Where is Doris?" Mom asked him.

"She went down to Houston to see her brother. He's not doing well. He got that cancer again, and this time the radiation ain't working like last time."

"Oh my," Mom said. "I hope he won't be in much pain."

"Me too," Luke said.

"When are you expecting her back?" Dad asked.

"Tomorrow morning. Though she said she might stay another day. If she shows up tomorrow, we'll know that this," he waved his hand skyward, "didn't get all the way down to Houston."

"Why are all the lights out, Pat?" Mom asked. She had a look of mild confusion on her face,

"We are having a blackout, Dear. It might be out for a couple of days."

"Oh. I don't know what's wrong with me, I have been tired all day. Is there anything I can fix for ya'll to eat?"

Luke cocked his head to the side as if considering. "I think I ate enough of your food tonight, Abbey. I'm afraid if you fix me anything else, I'll explode."

"That's good, Luke. I never want you to go hungry. I think I'll go check on Doris. Is she still in the restroom?"

"I don't think so, Abbey. Maybe you can just sit and rest. When she gets here, I'll send her into the living room."

"Oh, I have too much to do to be sitting all night," Mom said to Luke with a shake of her head. "And besides, I think Doris is still in Houston."

Luke scratched his thick beard the way he always did when he was worried about something.

"You're right, Abbey," Dad said. "Luke was just telling us about Doris' trip to Houston. Remember the water is off."

Mom was putting dishes into the sink as Dad was talking to her. When he mentioned the water was off she spun around.

"I remember! Do you think I don't?"

I had a clear recollection of Mom yelling at me that way when I was a teenager. I never expected to hear her yell at Dad that way.

"I know you remember," he said. "I was just thinking out loud."

"Well maybe you should keep those damn thoughts to yourself!"

She slammed the plate she was holding onto the countertop and turned and walked out of the room. The door to their bedroom slammed shut a few seconds later.

"Sorry about that, Luke," Dad said softly.

"No worries, Pat. I watched my mother go through it. Was not happy to hear her swear, though. Mom didn't swear until she was starting to get real bad."

"It started a few weeks ago. She cursed me up a blue streak when I asked for butter for the toast. Haven't heard that kind of talk since I was in the Navy."

I sat at the table and didn't say anything. I tried hard not to think about Mom slipping away, but Dad and Luke talking about it openly made it seem real in a way I hadn't dealt with before.

"Davey, sorry. I can see this is upsetting you," Dad said. "Let's talk about what we are going to need to do about this disruption to our lives."

"Folks are going to die, you know," Luke said.

"I know," Dad replied. "That's another reason we need the wood ash."

"Graves," I muttered. "We need to line the graves with ashes because we can't embalm the bodies."

"A layer below and a layer above," Luke said. "We dig down deep enough to bury them proper and we run the risk of contaminating the ground water. Same with the privies."

"How many privies will we need to dig?" I asked.

Luke and Dad both leaned back in their chair.

"Maybe one for every eight people," Dad said.

Luke closed his eyes tight and scratched his beard again. "We got about three thousand people in town. Maybe another five hundred that will make their way in. So maybe four hundred privies. That won't be a one day job."

"How deep do they have to be?" I asked.

"Normally six feet," Dad said. "But for now, we could dig them three feet for the next couple of days and then set about getting the six footers dug."

"I take it you are seeing this thing last more than a couple of weeks," Luke said. It seemed a question, but one he had answered while asking.

Dad nodded and looked at me.

"What did Ted say, Davey? Did he give any indication about what's happening?"

"Solar flare from last night is what he believes happened," I said.

Luke grunted. "Good. Would hate to think someone would have been stupid enough to hit us with a weapon."

Dad shook his head. "No, not good, Luke. If it were a weapon, it would be fairly localized. I suspect most of the world got hit with the effects. I wonder how far south people can see those lights. If the flare was big enough, it might have lit up the whole world."

"How long do you think it will last?" I asked.

"Not sure," Dad said. "Don't really know why it's happening."

"Enjoy it tonight," Luke said. "Last night, the weatherman out of Poplar Bluff said we have a storm front heading our way in the next couple of days. Clouds will make tomorrow night darker than most people are used to."

"So what do we do now?" I asked. I didn't really expect an answer.

"Listen to Ted," Luke said. "He's probably planned all of this out. I suspect he and Lester Collins both have a year's worth of food and water stockpiled for themselves. Surprised Ted came into town to help, to be honest. Folks always treated him quite unkindly anytime he started talking about emergency planning."

"Chicken Little is what most people said about him and Lester. Always saying the sky was going to fall and they were going to be ready when it did," Dad added.

"I guess they were right," I said. I tried to sound as sagely as both of the gray haired men I was sitting with. I think I succeeded because both of them nodded as they looked down at their hands.

"I guess the first thing we need to do is get the wells and privies taken care of," Luke said after a little silence. "Then we need to worry about food."

"Yeah, I figure we have probably three or four days per family in the cupboards and pantries around here," Dad said.

"What about any stores? They must have some."

"Nope, they shut up the market a few years back. And even so, they would only have a day or two worth for three thousand mouths," Luke said.

"Stews and soups for a while," said Dad. "We will need to stretch what we have as far as we can."

"How fast can we grow food?" I asked. "Like beans and corn?"

"Not sure. How about it, Luke? Can we grow food fast enough?" Dad asked.

"Onions, radishes maybe. Lettuce grows pretty quick, I think. We can start seeing what vegetable seeds people have."

"Anyone with a big garden?" I asked.

"Milton," Dad said. "He sells crops at the farmer's market in West Plains all the time. His garden runs five acres or so."

"It won't be enough to feed the town," Luke said.

"No, but he'll have plenty of seeds," I said.

Luke nodded. "And he'll know what crops we can start growing and in what order."

"It's getting late," Dad said as he yawned. "I did more physical work today than I have in a long time. I need to get to sleep."

"Mind if I crash on your couch?" Luke asked. "I'm pretty tired too and my house is a good mile away."

"Go ahead," Dad answered. "We are supposed to meet the others here tomorrow morning, might as well already be here."

I stood and stretched. "I may not have reopened wells today, but I am tired just the same."

"Night, Davey. I'm going to help Luke get settled in and will be back in a bit."

I walked down the hall towards my old bedroom. The glowing sky cast odd shadows as I walked down a path I had taken hundreds of times. Even in the pitch black, I would have been able to traverse the way with no problems, but the shimmering light with a pale greenish hue, seemed to disorient me.

Once in the room I closed the door and sat on the bed. As I took off my shoes, my eyes fell on my old desk. The top was arranged with several pieces of high school memorabilia. The tassel from my graduation cap hung on the corner of a framed picture of my senior photo. I always carried a pack of gum in my front shirt pocket and… my pocket watch.

I stood and opened the top drawer of the desk. Inside was a jumble of items, most of which I never remembered owning. But near the bottom of that pile was a pocket watch. Or should be.

I rooted around until I found it. It was a simple pocket watch. My grandfather had bought it for me when I was ten years old. I carried it with me until I went to college.

I pressed the button that opened the case. Inside was a photo of me and my grandfather on my tenth birthday.

He passed away of a heart attack two weeks after that day. It's why the watch had meant so much to me.

How many years had it been since I had thought about him for more than a passing moment? How many years had it been since I felt the sadness I remembered as a child for his passing?

I pulled out on the button a bit and wound the watch. As I was still winding, I heard the comforting sound of the watch start running. The mechanical aspect of the watch was affected by the EMP as much as a hinge on a door was.

I smiled as I realized what we needed to do was focus on what still worked and not despair over what didn't. If I could keep accurate time by winding a watch, what else could we do if we just stepped back a few decades and did things as they used to be done?

I undressed for bed as I considered that. For all of the concern and uncertainty, my dad and his friends got things accomplished today. They may have been worried, but they did more than worry. They did something. I feared my generation and the ones that followed liked to talk about what we would do, or should do, but we rarely did anything.

I finished winding the watch and set it on the desk. Sleep beckoned to me and I undressed and slipped under the covers. A few minutes later I heard my dad walk down the hallway and go into his bedroom.

I lay there and listened to the sounds around me. The sound of my dad moving about in his room. Luke trying to get comfortable in the living room. I listened for the sounds of the animals, but there were none. Last night the lights caused them to go wild. Tonight it seemed as if the animals felt too tired to make noise. It was quiet except for the ticking of my watch.

I drifted off considering that. A small sound in a quiet place grows in volume, it seems. The sound brought back memories of my grandfather. And then thoughts of Lexi and Emma. I had tried not to think of them all day. I hoped they were alright. I prayed somehow Chicago was spared this event. I knew there was nothing I could do, so I tried not to worry about them.

I drifted asleep trying not to worry. My dreams took me to them. I saw my greatest hopes and my greatest fears for them played out. And I walked and talked with my grandfather.

SIX

I woke the next morning to the smell of bacon and coffee. It took me a few minutes to orient myself to where I was and what had happened.

Emma and Lexi had been in my dreams. They were calling for help, but I couldn't find them.

Tears welled up in my eyes as the emotions of the dreams still lingered. After a quick prayer for their safety, I rolled out of bed and got dressed.

I needed a shower, but knew that wasn't going to happen, so I made my way into the kitchen and waved at Dad. He was flipping through a notebook when I came in. Mom was cooking at the stove. I wasn't sure how much liquid propane was in the old tank out back, but I was grateful Mom still had the ability to make breakfast for us.

"David," Mom said as I approached the table. "I have eggs and bacon and some hash browns. I'll get you some coffee, but it will have to be black. We don't have any milk, but that's probably for the best as the refrigerator isn't working."

"Thanks, Mom," I said as I sat at the table.

"If you need to wash up, I have a couple of five gallon buckets of water in the garage," Dad said as Mom put my breakfast in front of me.

"Where did you get those?" I asked.

"Well, not all of us sleep in past dawn," Dad said with a smile. "I went and got water from the well."

"You carried a five gallon bucket of water across the street?" I asked.

Dad sniffed. "It's not that heavy."

"Dad. Look at me."

He sighed and looked up from his papers.

I sat my fork down and tried to look at him like he was Emma. "You know the doctors said you were to not to be moving things more than twenty pounds. I realize you probably did a lot of digging and moving of things yesterday you weren't supposed to, but I don't want to hear of any more of that kind of activity."

"Okay, Pops," Dad said.

His mockery cut a bit, but I knew he needed to be told he was being watched.

"Five gallons of water is close to forty pounds, and you know that."

"That's why I only carried one bucket at a time."

"Well now you need to only carry a gallon at a time, or wait for me to get the water."

"David," Mom said. "He was only doing what he thought he should."

"I'm sorry, Dad. And I know, Mom. I'm just concerned."

"Shush," Dad said as he looked at me with a sharp expression.

"Pat, don't talk to David like that."

Dad held his finger up to his lips as a sign she should be quiet as well.

I was irritated at his refusal to listen to me, but then I realized he was listening to something else. When I realized what it was, I jumped to my feet and ran to the front door. Dad was just a step behind me.

When I pulled open the door, the sound was clear and distinct. Someone was using a motorized weed trimmer.

"It's Bill Jenner," Dad said. "He is out trimming his house. Look."

I looked to where Dad pointed and saw a rotund, balding man holding a weed whacker, trimming the weeds from around a bush near the side of his house.

As if drawn to the sound, I started walking toward Bill Jenner's house, three lots over. I noticed there were others outside of their houses beyond the spectacle. Because Bill was on our side of his house, the others were looking around in astonishment.

As I walked toward Jenner and his amazing activity, I noticed two horses were headed my way down Granger. Anne would be here soon with both of her horses, but I had to find out what was happening.

I looked behind me and the Johnson's were out of their house looking our way. Sarah had her phone out and looked at it with a furious visage. I guess she thought if one machine was working, the rest had to be as well.

Bill looked over his shoulder as we approached. I could see by his blood-shot eyes and sallow complexion he wasn't feeling real well that morning. He was sweating more than even a heavy man should on a cool April morning. He was hung-over.

Dad and I stopped at the edge of his lawn and just watched him. Soon, a small crowd of people were gathered around. No one spoke. We were mesmerized by the sound and sight of a machine working.

Bill worked around the back of his house and then up the other side. All the while, a crowd of people lined his yard in the front. He took glances over at the crowd occasionally, but kept about his work.

Finally he was done and he turned off the trimmer. The spell was broken and people started talking. Some took out their phones, like Sarah had, and started trying to turn them on. It disturbed me a little that so many people were so attached to their phones that they still had them in their pockets two days after they had becomes useless chunks of plastic and metal. Maybe they held hope that somehow this situation would just resolve itself.

Bill walked into his garage and put his trimmer up. He climbed on his riding mower and tried to start it. Nothing happened. He tried again. He looked out at the crowd lining his property and then dropped his face into his hands. I guess he finally remembered what had happened. He climbed down from his mower and went into his house.

As his door closed, the crowd broke up.

"Isn't that a sight," Anne said.

"I think we need to figure out if any of my tools might work," Dad said as we walked back to the house. "You start looking in the garage, I'll go get the key to the shed."

"What should we be looking for?" I asked.

"We're supposed to go into town, David," Anne said.

"Anything gas powered to start. We'll check anything with batteries as well, but I'm not optimistic about those," Dad answered.

I wanted to follow Dad, but Anne required attention first.

"Anne, let Ted know what happened here, okay?"

"Do you want me to leave Clyde here for you?"

"No," I said. "Take him into town and see if someone else can use him?"

"Okay, I'll let Ted know. And when I get done, I'll come back for supper."

"Why?" I asked. It sounded short and rude, but I didn't understand why she would want to come back to my house for supper.

"Because it's been a few months since I have spent time with your folks. Just because you threw me out of your life doesn't mean they did."

She mounted Bonnie and led Clyde north into town. I could feel the embarrassment coloring my face.

I went into the garage and started looking carefully at everything in there. Most of the things I found were hand tools or gardening equipment. The few power tools I found were electric.

I joined Dad out in the shed after half an hour of searching the garage.

"Find anything?" he asked.

I shook my head. "No. Found two flashlights, but neither worked."

"Those probably need new batteries."

"I was wondering about the flashlight that didn't work the first night," I said. "Seems the EMP didn't fry the smoke detector battery, so why should it have hurt the ones in the flashlight?"

"That one is an LED flashlight," Dad said. "I figure the EMP hit the display, not the batteries. The ones in the garage are the old incandescent type. If the bulbs didn't pop when the pulse went through, they should be okay."

Dad had a keen mind and I was always amazed at how quick he was to come to a correct conclusion.

"Find anything out here?" I asked.

"Acetylene torch, small chainsaw, and roto-tiller. Those are the only ones I have hope for."

I looked at the equipment he named and reached for the chainsaw when I heard a horse approaching. I looked out expecting to see Anne riding back. I would have a chance to apologize for my insensitive comment. But instead I saw Ted on a splotchy brown and white horse.

"Morning," Ted said as he dismounted. "Heard there was some excitement here a little while back."

My Dad stepped out of the shed and looked at the man who had brought some semblance of order in town yesterday.

"Ted, nice to see you again."

"You too, Pat. David here said he was going to be my runner for this section. I was surprised he was your son, as easy as he was to work with."

Dad chuckled a little, walked over to Ted, and stuck out his hand.

"No hard feelings?"

Ted shook my dad's hand and smiled. "None, Pat. Calling me a paranoid nut-job who can do what he wants is one of the nicer receptions I've had in this town."

"Yeah. Well, I guess you get the last laugh."

Ted shook his head. "No, this is nothing to laugh about. I just want to keep as many people alive as possible."

"You think it's long term?" Dad asked.

"Maybe. But we better plan on that being the case. We won't have a lot of time otherwise."

"Dad and some of the others have already started planning," I said.

"I heard about that," Ted said turning toward me. "Wells reopened and a big bonfire last night."

"Wood ash," Dad said simply.

"Means latrines, then," Ted said. "Good, that gives me a little less to worry about. Sounds like the south section is being taken care of."

"And graves," Dad said.

Ted looked back at him. "And graves. I hope we don't need them soon, but we need to lay in as much ash as we can. One outbreak and we will need it by the ton."

"A bad enough outbreak…" Dad lifted his hands as he let the thought drift by.

A small crowd was starting to gather where we were standing. Most of the neighbors had heard me say Ted had taken charge in town, and now he was here a few miles south of the town itself, they were curious to hear what he had to say.

"I better go check on my wife, Ted," Dad said as he motioned to the gathering people. "You have an audience it looks like."

I hesitated between going with Dad and staying with Ted. As neither man indicated what I should do, I decided I would go in the house and let Ted deal with the questions by himself.

I went through the garage and into the kitchen. I heard my parents in the living room. Mom was upset and Dad was trying to calm her down.

"It's okay, Abbey. I'll pick it up."

"I wasn't upset or anything, Pat. I just forgot the power was out and when the vacuum wouldn't come on… I was putting it up when I bumped the table. That's how the table got knocked over."

"I know, that table has been in my way many times"

I watched from the back of the kitchen. This was something I had tried to ignore for several years now. I couldn't imagine how Dad kept it together like this day after day.

Dad set the table back to where it was and Mom picked up the bowl, doily, and other items that had been sitting on top. She gave them to Dad and then carefully put away the vacuum cleaner.

"David," she said as she looked into the kitchen. "I thought you were outside."

"I was, but I wanted to see if you needed anything else."

"I don't think so," she answered. "Pat? Is there anything you need David to do?"

Dad looked up at me. His eyes were rimmed in red and he let out a long sigh.

"Thanks. Would you mind getting a clean five-gallon bucket from the shed and go get more water? Your mom wants to boil a few potatoes for dinner, and we will need to get that started soon."

"Sure, Dad," I said. I waited until Mom had taken the vacuum down to the hall closet before I walked into the living room.

"Is there anything else I can do?" I asked as I drew near to him.

He stood from his work on the table and shook his head. "No, this is a good day, all things considered."

"Okay," I said. I left the house through the kitchen door and went through the garage to the shed. The crowd around Ted and his horse seemed in a good mood. Hearing what had to be done was one thing, hearing it from someone who had authority behind him was something else.

I went to the shed and found several five gallon buckets stacked together. I pulled one free of the collection and walked past the crowd toward the street.

"Hey stranger, Dad have you working all day?"

I turned to see Anne riding toward me on Bonnie. Kenny was behind her riding Clyde. He looked very ill at ease on top of the horse.

"We looked for anything that might work. I expect most people around here wasted the morning doing that."

"Find anything good?"

"A few items might work. They run on gas. But Ted got here before we could test them."

"Anne, I need to get off your horse now," Kenny insisted.

I set my bucket down on the side of the road and took Clyde's reins. I offered a hand to Kenny, but he just tumbled from the back of Clyde almost knocking me down as he fell.

"You okay?" I asked.

"Yeah," he said. "Just don't like riding. Told her, told Ted and now I'm telling you."

I helped him to his feet and tried not to smile too much at his discomfort.

"Good to see you again, Kenny."

"You too, David. I need to go help Ted now."

I watched as Kenny dashed across my yard to attend to Ted.

"Everything go okay in town?" I asked Anne.

"Yeah, Ted really knows what to do. Wells and latrines were the two big items on his list today. Sounds like your dad and his buddies were on the right track yesterday. What are you doing?" She nodded as I picked the bucket back up.

"Mom needs some water for dinner, so I'm going to the well to get some."

"I need someone to come out and get my well working again. I have some bottled water left, and there is a water tank for the animals that was filled last week, thank God."

"Do you have anyone who can fix that for you?" I asked.

"I don't know, I'll ask around today. I guess we will be pushing wells and food rationing."

"And latrines. And wood ash for the latrines."

She wrinkled her nose.

"What a great topic to bring up to people. But, it's better than them not knowing."

"Go on to the house," I said. "I will get the water and be back in a few minutes."

Anne led the horses to my parent's front door and I turned back to my chore. The well was about sixty feet from the road and surrounded by people. Several adults and a few children waited in line to pump water from the old Anderson well. A few of the women kept looking at the crowd around Ted. Their anxiety was clear as they waited their turn for fresh water. I'm sure they were all curious at what he was telling their husbands.

By the time I was able to fill the bucket and start back across the street, the crowd around Ted was breaking up. I was surprised at how heavy the bucket was after it was filled with water. I would definitely prohibit Dad from fetching any more himself.

As I staggered up the side of the ditch to the road, I heard the unmistakable roar of a motorcycle. I had to shield my eyes from the bright afternoon sun as I looked to the south. There came a man on a motorcycle that sped toward town. As he passed, I could hear him yell in a sort of victory roar. He turned around about a mile later and came back.

This time, when the crowds came to marvel at what had been normal two days prior, they were not stunned into silence. They yelled and waved and jumped up and down. Men and women, grandparents and children, they all celebrated some guy on a motorcycle.

I pulled myself out of the ditch and onto the shoulder of the road. I was stronger than I was a few minutes before. I stood taller. I looked at the sky, with its slight shimmery waves of greens and blues, and smiled. The pulse of energy may have knocked us down, but for at least today, it hadn't knocked us out.

I crossed the street and brought the bucket of water into the house.

"Did you see that?" Anne asked as I came in.

"Yes, who is it?"

"I don't know," Dad said. "I think he moved into the Mitchell's place a couple of years ago. I saw him in the crowd at Bill's this morning. He must have realized he never checked to see if his motorcycle would work."

"Wow," said Ted as he stood in the front doorway. I had left the door open when I brought in the water.

"That was something, alright," Anne said. "I brought the horse over for David, but maybe that guy could be used since he has some real transportation."

EMP   Wilson Harp

"We'll find a way to use him," Ted said. "You guys ready to spread the word of what needs to be done today?"

"Yes," I said as Anne nodded.

"Good. Let me add an extra bit for everyone. Tonight people need to set out any clean buckets or containers they can. We might get some rain in here, and we want to gather as much water as possible. But remind them any water they drink or cook with needs to be boiled for ten minutes first."

"Got it," said Anne as she noted what he said on a slip of paper.

"Great. You two need to get going, I'd like to have a chat with Pat if I could."

I looked back at Dad. "You need me for anything else?"

"No, Davey. You go do what you need to, I'll take it easy today."

I looked over at Mom who was peeling potatoes in the kitchen.

"Okay," I said. "I'll be home in time for supper."

SEVEN

The rains came in little pulses over the next several days. Storms tore through the first night, darkening Kenton in a way I had never experienced. The northern lights were blocked out by the heavy clouds and the wind howled all the louder for the loss of sight.

The next two days saw a series of short showers. It brought plenty of fresh water to us, but delayed construction of individual latrines and outhouses. It also brought a melancholy that combined with worry and uncertainty.

A bright dawn greeted us on the third day and the sky looked clear in the north and west. The northern lights which had hung in the sky like specters the first two days were gone. Occasionally I would see a ribbon of color out of the corner of my eye, but it seemed more like a phantom feeling one would experience when they saw a bug and then lost track of it. A sensation would run along your leg or shoulder, but you knew it wasn't really there.

Anne arrived about an hour after sunup with Clyde for me to ride. The gelding was starting to get used to me and for the first time seemed to recognize me as I approached.

"Not wearing your coat and hat today?" Anne asked. She smirked as she kept any tone of mocking out of her voice. I had been forced to wear an old jacket and baseball cap from my high school years during the last couple of days just to stay somewhat dry.

"No, it's going to be a beautiful day," I said.

"Ready to head in and get orders from Ted?" she asked.

"I will later. I just want to check up on a few families and make sure they are boiling their water before they drink it," I said.

"I understand, I need to check on a few people myself. See you in town around lunch?"

"Okay."

Anne waved at me and turned Bonnie away as I mounted Clyde. I rode south along Granger until I came to the Carter's Creek Bridge. Just before that was a little spur of a road with three houses and a couple of mobile homes. One of those mobile homes had a single mother with three young children, and I wanted to make certain she was boiling any water before she mixed it with formula for her baby or powder mix for her older kids.

As I approached her house, I heard a commotion and saw an older man step out of a farmhouse that had been the only house in this area when I was growing up. He wailed a mournful cry and fell to his knees.

The Gatewood family had left the town soon after I graduated high school, so I wasn't familiar with the man who was crying on his front porch. I turned Clyde toward the house and dismounted as I approached the front gate. I opened the gate and ran up to the porch.

"What's wrong?" I asked.

"She's gone. She's gone," he muttered.

A few of his neighbors were gathering, including Luke Carter. I tried to get the man to focus on me, but tears had been on his cheeks and wetting his beard for some time before he had come outside.

Luke pushed past me and entered the house. The woman I was going to see about the water knelt beside the older man and hugged him.

A few minutes later, Luke came back out the front door. He motioned for me and another man who had come into the yard to join him at the bottom of the steps to the porch.

"Wanda is dead," he said.

"His wife?" I asked.

Luke nodded. "You might want to go let the council know."

The council was a group of six prominent and effective leaders in Kenton. Ted had selected them two nights before. He led the council and was supported by Mayor Mueller, John Laffer, Bill Hanson, Susan Skinner, Ike Stokes, and Clint Davis.

"Okay," I said. "Her name is Wanda, what is his."

"Kevin Cummings," said the other man.

"Why are you down this far, David?" Luke asked me. "I've got everything under control down here."

I pointed to the woman who was comforting the older man on the porch. "I was just coming down here to make sure she was boiling the water for her kids. I wasn't intending any offense, Mister Carter."

Luke smiled and dropped a heavy arm on my shoulder.

"You are so much like your dad. There is no offense, you're doing the job they gave you. I'll take care of it. You go let the council know we had a death overnight. I think she died in her sleep. I figure we can give Kevin the day to deal with it and then tonight we can dig the grave and bury her."

I mounted Clyde and rode away from the tragic scene. I didn't want to stop by the house and speak with my folks. I told myself it was because I didn't want Dad to feel like he had to get involved, but I knew I just didn't want to cry. And if I spoke to my folks about it, I would cry. It wasn't fair. I hadn't cried over being unable to help Lexi and Emma, but I would cry over some woman I had never met. I knew I would cry, and I knew that wasn't fair somehow.

As I kicked around those thoughts in my head, I rode past the house and was able to ride into town dry-eyed.

I entered the library, which had become the headquarters for our efforts. Maps of the town were laid out on the large tables, and Ted had more volunteers than he knew what to do with.

Mayor Mueller was an invaluable asset to Ted, and I could see why he was in his fifth term. He was an efficient administrator and could handle people and their complaints in a smooth and confident manner. But he had met his match in Sharon Little.

"I don't know, Missus Little," the mayor said. "I don't have the resources to check on that for you."

"It's 'Miz Little', and you can't tell me if there is a single milk goat in this town?"

"I'm sorry Miz Little. I don't know. I don't drink goat milk."

"This is unbelievable! I can't feed my children because of your incompetence?"

"You don't need to shout—"

"Yes I do! I need everyone to know you are completely useless! What are we supposed to do?"

I was a taken aback by this outburst as I walked through the door of the main meeting room. The other people in the room had all stopped what they were doing and watched the confrontation. A sudden drop in the noise in the main library had me look over my shoulder. Most people had stopped what they were working on and some were edging over to look through the door.

"Miz Little, your children will be fine. We still have enough food here in town," said the mayor. "The hunting is going well and we have several large plots of radishes that will be harvested in the next couple of weeks. We may have to tighten our belts for a bit, but we will get through this."

"The only thing I've seen anyone offer me this morning is prepackaged food and dried meat."

The mayor blinked a couple of times. "I don't understand your concern, then. Is the goat milk important to your children's diet? If so, Bill Hanson can recommend a way to help their digestion. He may have some medicine that could help."

Sharon threw her hands up in the air and made a mocking sound. "It's not just the goat milk. I won't let my children eat the poison that is prepackaged food. And I certainly won't have them eating meat. We only eat holistic, healthy, all natural foods. And you need to find a source of them."

"I'll see what I can do. Perhaps you would like to volunteer to work at one of the community gardens to help with the crops, then. Shall I put you down?"

Mayor Mueller picked up a clipboard from the table and pulled a pen out of his pocket.

"Those crops are genetically modified, I'm sure. And I saw pesticides being used in those gardens," she said.

Sharon turned away from the mayor and stormed toward the doorway. I stepped out of her way, but apparently a small crowd had gathered behind me and she was forced to shove her way out of the meeting room.

The mayor shook his head as she left, then he turned to me.

"David, good to see you. Ted has something he wants some help with. He told me to grab you or Anne when you came in."

"Sounds like he needs a horse more than me or Anne," I said.

The mayor laughed. "Most likely so. He rode in today himself, so it probably is about a horse."

"I came in a little early today, mayor. I need to report something to the council."

"What is it, David?"

"We had a death last night in the south section."

"What happened?"

"Not sure. Wanda Cummings. Looks like she died in her sleep."

Mayor Mueller nodded. "Wanda and Kevin go to my church over in Low Springs. I can't imagine what he is going through."

"Luke went and looked at her. He said they would let Kevin have the day, then prepare and bury her tonight."

"Good. I knew there would be deaths, I was just hoping they wouldn't start so soon."

"There were others?"

"Yes, two others have been reported. One in town and one to the east. Both elderly."

"Stress?" I asked

"I think so. Ted was telling me this yesterday. He said as people accepted the situation, they would start to give up. Having no hope is a horrible stress to the system."

"That's right," a voice from behind me said.

I turned to see Ted standing behind me. He had a rifle slung over his shoulder. A canteen shared space on his heavy belt with a holstered pistol and a long handled knife.

"You—you wanted to see me Ted?" I stuttered as I took in the sight of him. He hadn't openly carried weapons since that first day in the square, and I was unsure what had prompted him to start today.

"You know how to shoot, David?" he asked.

I nodded. "Yeah, but it's been quite a while. If you are looking for a hunter, there are plenty better candidates. I can ask Anne if she will loan them Clyde if you need a shooter on a horse. Or Anne herself might be a good one to choose."

"I don't need a hunter, David. Just someone who can shoot if we get in a jam. I'm going out to see Lester and if things go well, I'll need the extra horse to bring back some stuff. If things go bad, I don't want to take anyone out who doesn't have at least a passing familiarity with a long gun."

"Lester Collins?" I asked.

"You know him?"

I shook my head. "No, but my dad and Luke mentioned him when this first started. Said he and you were both survivalists that…" I let my words drift out as I tried to make it less offensive.

"…that were derided and mocked?" Ted finished.

He was serious. There was no smile or edge of humor in his face. He could have eased the tension, but he didn't. He just left me to twist in the wind and choke on my words.

"Yes. They said most folks thought of you two as Chicken Littles, always proclaiming that the end was near."

Ted looked away and walked over to the mayor. "Carl, would you say that is a fair assessment of how me and Lester were viewed in this town?"

Mayor Mueller nodded. His grasp of diplomacy was better than mine and he kept his lips firmly shut.

"What do you think now, David? Was it just dumb luck or foresight that allowed me to prepare?"

"I think you are probably one of those people who always think the worst is going to happen and put faith in your pessimism."

Ted nodded. "Good enough. Let's mount up."

"You could ask Buck Fredrickson, I'll give him my horse if you need someone."

"Do you not want to go, David?" Ted asked.

"No, I just thought you would want the right man for the job."

Ted looked at me for a few seconds. He locked his eyes on mine. I felt like looking away, but I held firm.

"Buck and his guys are out hunting. They brought down two deer the first day, but now they are only bringing in a couple of rabbits and squirrels. And they are good hunters. Very good."

He stepped closer to me.

"Do you have any idea why the bigger game has suddenly disappeared from the area?" he asked.

"No," I said. "I wouldn't have a clue."

"Buck doesn't know either, but he is still out searching for meat for the town. I need him out there doing that, and I need you for this job. Besides, Buck and Lester hate each other and I would have a shoot-out on my hands if I took him. We'll leave when you are ready."

He walked out of the meeting room without another word.

"Deputy McDaniels still doesn't trust him and I don't know if I do fully," Mayor Mueller said. "But I do know he has a plan and that's better than the rest of us."

"That's what Dad says, too." I said as I looked at the doorway long after Ted had left.

"It's a shame your dad turned down a position on the council. I know Ted really wanted him on board once he heard the south section had already uncapped wells and were preparing wood ash for latrines and graves," said the mayor. "Ted doesn't seem to be impressed easily, but your dad sure impressed him."

"My mom... she needs my dad to be with her as much as possible."

"You better get out there. Don't want to make Ted impatient."

I left the library and was mounting up on Clyde when Ted came around the side of the library mounted on his own horse. He reined in close to me and handed me a rifle.

"You ever use one of those before?"

It was an older Winchester. Lever action. Thirty caliber. My dad had one like it when I was a kid.

"Yeah, I've shot a rifle like this a few times."

"Okay, just a quick refresher from Colonel Cooper. All guns are loaded. Even when you know they aren't. Never cover anything with the barrel you don't want to destroy. Never put your finger on the trigger until you are ready to fire. Never fire until you are sure what is behind your target. Keep those rules in mind and there will be no gun accidents."

I nodded as I slung the rifle over my neck and shoulder. "I'll remember. Just don't do anything that will make me have to use this."

Ted rode forward and I urged Clyde to follow. Several people stared at us as we rode out of town, but no one seemed too distraught over having a couple of armed men ride past them. What a difference a week made.

When we turned north on Line Ave, I heard the sound of a lawnmower. I smiled and rode up next to Ted. I pointed at the two boys watching a man mow his yard.

"Yeah," Ted said. "I guess most people are still amazed at what is working."

We rode north until we left town, and then turned down a small drive to the east. It wasn't anywhere I was familiar with, and I wondered who lived out this way. Never found out. Ted rode off the drive and out into a field between some twisted sections of barbed wire fencing that no longer created an effective barrier to travel.

"Hey!"

I turned in my saddle and brought Clyde to a stop with the reins. I heard Ted do the same with his mount. I looked back to see where the call had come from, but the trees were too heavy to see far.

Anne came out of the tree line and trotted over to us on Bonnie.

"I didn't expect you to head off the road," Anne said as she approached. "What are you doing with rifles?"

"We're heading to see Lester," Ted answered.

"Why? Do you think he might actually help?"

"Maybe," Ted said. "Kenny left for his place this morning on foot with a big white pillowcase to wave at Lester's front drive. Hopefully he will have talked with Kenny and we will be able to get a few things."

"What does he have?" I asked.

"Water purification tablets. A good supply of seeds. Maybe some antibiotics if we are lucky. And, unless his cage failed as well, a shortwave radio."

"What do you mean 'his cage'?" I asked.

"A Faraday cage. It's a grounded enclosure that directs electrical fields around whatever is inside it. I had a shortwave radio in my cage, but it still got fried."

"How is that possible?" Anne asked.

Ted shrugged. "Not sure. But I intend to try to fix it, unless Lester lets us use his."

"We aren't going to find out just talking in this field," I said. "Let's get going and see what happens."

Ted turned his horse and rode across the field. Anne and I took up positions on either side of him.

"Why were you following us, Anne?" Ted asked.

"Mayor Mueller told me which way you were headed. I have some news you need to know."

"What's that?"

"Hank Kroner killed himself last night. Left a note."

"I don't know him," Ted said. "Was I mentioned in the note?"

"No. Hank is… was a man in his eighties. He shot himself in the head. The note said we were to use anything and everything he had left to help other people survive."

Ted shook his head and grimaced. "I was afraid this would happen."

"What?" I asked.

"Older people in particular can start to feel useless when something like this hits. Especially when they don't have any family close by." Ted turned to Anne. "He didn't have any family, did he?"

"Not near, no," she answered.

"So he looks around and says "Why should I be using up all of this water and food? I'm not going to be around much anymore." Then he puts a gun in his mouth and does the noble thing."

"How do we stop that from spreading?" Anne asked.

"The pragmatist in me says we shouldn't. But I suggest moving older people who are by themselves in with families that have young children. We can tell them the older people can keep an eye on the kids, which will free up the stronger adults to do more robust work. Like helping with the crops."

A gunshot cracked in the distance. The loud ranting of Ted was mute by comparison. We all galloped forward. Toward the sound of the gunfire. Toward Lester Collins' house.

EIGHT

Lester lived in a modest ranch style house on a plot of land that had a grove of walnut trees on one side, and a thick hedge of brushy cedars growing around the rest of the property. The only access road big enough for a car went through a heavy steel cattle gate that was set into the heavy line of cedars.

Crouched off to the side of the gate was Kenny. He was sweating heavily and had a white pillowcase clutched in his hand. When we turned from the field on the road that led to the gate, Kenny looked back at us and waved us away from the gate.

"Is that you, Ted?" A voice shouted the question from a good distance beyond the gate.

We rode off the side of the road up to Kenny. The high brush line giving us plenty of cover from the house.

"It's me, Les," Ted yelled back as he dismounted. "Were you shooting at Kenny?"

"Not at him," Lester yelled back. "I just told him to step away from the gate and when he didn't, I fired into the ground."

"Bullets ricochet, you stupid redneck," Kenny yelled.

Ted put a hand on Kenny's shoulder and motioned him to join Anne and me. We had dismounted and moved the horses even farther away from the road.

"I saw three ride up, Ted. Who you got with you?"

"Anne Franklin and David Hartsman."

"Who?"

"He's visiting his folks. He grew up in Kenton."

A few seconds passed before Lester answered. "Is he a cop?"

Ted rolled his eyes and shook his head. "He's not a cop and no one cares about what you're growing. We need some help."

Lester laughed and snorted. "I bet you do. What did you fail to prepare for?"

"I need some water tabs."

"Water tabs? I know you have a bunch. I saw you buy them."

"Yeah," Ted yelled. "And we need more. We have almost enough wells reopened, but the water isn't drawing from deep enough yet. We will need more tabs. And antibiotics."

"Wait a second. Are you telling me you are helping the town?"

"Yes, Lester. The town needs help, so that is what I am doing."

"You have shit for brains, Riggins. You know how they treated us. You know what they thought about you."

"I know Les, but they will die if no one helps them."

"Then let them die! They deserve it."

"It's already started. And maybe they do deserve it, but I will do what I can to see as many people survive."

"Already? Disease?"

"No, some elderly."

"Suicides?"

Ted sighed. "One so far."

Lester didn't say anything after that. Anne started to move over to the gate after about ten minutes, but Ted motioned her back. After a few more minutes, the front door to the house opened.

"I'm coming out Ted, but I have Joey at the window with a rifle. Any funny stuff and we'll riddle you full of holes and then the town won't have anyone to help them."

"Fair enough, Les. I'll put down my stuff and stand in front of the gate."

"You do that." Lester was moving closer to the gate by the sound of his voice.

"What else do you need?" Lester asked as he drew near the gate.

"Seed," Ted said. "I know you have some squash, zucchini and wheat seed in quantity."

"I do," Lester said. "But here's the problem. Those are slow growing crops. I assume you have already planted your radishes, turnips and lettuce. So if you need the slow growers, you expect to be feeding a lot of people. And you have a supply of water tabs and antibiotics with your supply and the pharmacy, so you don't have an immediate need for those either."

"What are you getting at, Les?"

"You want something else. Something you need now. Otherwise you would have waited me out a few more weeks before you came begging. Now what is it?"

"I need to use your radio."

"What?"

"Your radio, Les. I won't take it, but I want to be able to use it. Once a week for fifteen minutes."

"That's a lot to ask for, Ted. What happened to yours?"

"Cage wasn't set up right, I guess. Completely fried."

"And what would you give me in exchange for use of my radio?"

"What would you want?"

I heard Lester spit on the ground. After a minute he spoke. "I'd want to use yours, of course. Cause my cage didn't hold either."

Ted turned his head towards us. His jaw was clenched and I could tell he was holding in an explosion.

"Alright, I guess we are in the same boat then, Les. What about the other stuff?"

"Well, here's what I can do for you. I'll trade you the seed today, seeing as how you need to get it into the ground. The other stuff can wait. You can come back in a month and we can see how things are going."

"Okay. What do you want for the seed?"

"I want as much of your crop as me and my boys need. And you have to replenish our seed out of the first crop."

"How many you got with you?"

"I'm not going to give away any raw numbers, Ted. You know me better than that. I don't want to have your townsfolk think they can just come in here and take what is mine."

"That isn't going to happen, Les."

"No, it won't."

"So we have a deal?"

"Almost. One thing we failed to consider when we set up our little survival plan was making sure we had enough female types to keep us happy."

"I'm not sending girls out here, Les. Forget it."

"No, you misunderstand. I just want you to spread the word that any woman who wants to come out here and enjoy our protection, our food, our weed, and our booze will be more than welcome."

Ted didn't say anything for a few minutes.

"Just let them know of our invitation, Riggins."

"Okay, but I want the seed now. I'll let the town know what you said."

"Good. Now where is Kenny? I want him to come in and get the seed."

"I'll get him," said Ted.

Ted walked over to Kenny and spoke quietly to him. Kenny nodded and went to the gate. The gate swung open just enough for Kenny to slip through.

"How many men do you figure he has?" Anne asked.

"Maybe ten or twelve."

"Are you going to tell the town of Lester's offer?" I asked.

"Of course he is," Anne said.

"What? Why?"

"Because it will be less mouths to feed, less people to take care of if some take him up on the offer."

"She's right," Ted said. "We are going to be dealing with drugs and booze, anyway. That is wasted energy trying to get work out of those who will want to step out of reality for a bit. Some of those girls and women will see his invitation as a way to survive with as little work as possible."

I couldn't believe what Ted said, but when I looked at Anne, she had the same calm resolve in her eyes that Ted had in his voice. An invitation would be made to any who would be interested.

"Ted," Kenny called from the gate. "I got the squash and zucchini seed. Lester is having some of his men bring the wheat bags.

"He try to get you to stay?" Ted asked.

"Yeah. Just like me and you talked about. They were smoking weed and had all of their booze lined up when I went in the barn. He means to party his way through the next couple of months."

"How many?"

"Twenty, maybe twenty-five men. About five women. All of them with one of the men."

Ted nodded. "That's twice as many as I was expecting. That's also why he wants more women. He didn't recruit enough of them."

"That's what I figure," Kenny said as he placed the seed bags on the ground. "They are armed to the teeth as well. I'm guessing they have enough to live on for a while, then they will start scavenging."

"Scavenging?" Anne asked.

"Yeah, what Les is counting on is some of the towns around here will collapse. Then he and his boys can go and gather up resources they need. And recruit some of the healthy survivors if they can," Ted said.

"He really believes this is the end of the world." Anne said. Her voice was a mix of disbelief and revulsion.

"Yep," Kenny said. "And he wants to go out at the very top. Now, any of ya'll want to help me get this seed loaded up on the horses?"

I walked over to where the seed bags were and tried to lift them both. It didn't happen. I never thought of myself as a weakling, but after struggling with the bucket of water the day before and now not being able to lift the bags Kenny had carried a hundred yards by himself, I realized I probably should have been hitting the weights more these last few years.

Kenny stretched and then took hold of the one of the bags. Together we secured them to the back of Ted's horse.

While we did, four men came down the drive from the house and delivered two huge sacks of wheat.

"Les says that will feed five thousand," one of the men said. "There is enough for two plantings. Hope you have the means to flour it."

One of the other men chuckled and spit on the ground. The other three turned and walked back to the house. The spitter closed the gate and locked it with a heavy lock.

Ted and Anne removed the saddles from Bonnie and Clyde and set them on the ground. Then they loaded one of the bags of grain onto Bonnie while Kenny and I loaded the other bag on Clyde. The horses didn't seem to mind the weight, and I figured as much as they were capable of carrying, it probably wasn't any different than having a rider on their back.

"Get the saddle and let's get going," Ted said. "I want to make town before noon if possible."

I looked at Anne. She already had her saddle up on her shoulder. She smiled and pointed at the saddle that had been on Clyde.

I sighed and picked up the saddle. It wasn't as heavy as the seed, but I knew I would be worn out by the time we got to town. I put it on my shoulder and tried not to think about how far it would be.

Kenny led both Bonnie and Clyde, which was a great relief to me.

"We need to get these crops in the ground as quickly as possible," Ted said. "We should have a few hundred pounds of radishes coming up in a couple of weeks. We can add some small game meat and make a stew, but we will need more substantial food."

"He said he hoped we could turn the wheat into flour. Can we?" Anne asked.

Kenny looked over to her. "We can, if folks will listen to what I tell them. I know how to grind out grains into flour, but we will have to do it by hand unless we can find a couple of millstones."

"Won't that take a lot of effort?" I asked. "I mean, more than it may be worth?"

Ted laughed. "You will never taste a better bite of bread than the first bite you take from a loaf you brought from seedling to oven."

"You've done it before, then?"

"Yep, that's why the town called us crazy. We prepared for a time like this."

"You're still crazy," said Anne. She smiled at Ted as she said it, though.

"That I am. And Lester. And Kenny. Maybe not Kenny. He actually went through an end of the world experience. Me and Lester, we just read about them and realized how horrible it would be should it happen."

"And based on what could happen, you built your life around it?" I asked.

"Well," Ted said, "if I could survive in a moneyless society based on barter and my skills, I knew I could survive in a society where money was easy to get and even easier to trade for what I wanted."

Kenny nodded. "It's easy to buy a pound of hamburger from a man when the piece of paper you give him will let him replace what he sold and leave him some profit. Try buying it when he can't replace it and his family will starve without it."

"I see what you mean," I said.

"So you decided since you could survive when there was a collapse, then you should be able to survive before there was one," Anne added.

"Correct," Ted confirmed.

"But didn't you want more than survival?" Anne asked.

"I did once," Kenny said. "I thought I could somehow have a big life. Fancy cars, big house, money would be no concern. Then Katrina done washed away all of those dreams. Good thing too, cause I wasn't heading to those things. I was barely surviving, but I didn't realize it."

"So what about after Katrina? What did you do?" I asked.

"My sister had her husband take off on her after she had her third, so I figured maybe she could use some help. Honestly, I needed help to, and I figured she might be able to get me enough cash to get back to New Orleans or maybe Atlanta and I could start over.

"But when I got here, she was just dirt poor. I asked why she wasn't on food stamps or assistance, and she slapped me. She asked me if I had no brains at all. I was mad, but she was my little sister, so I asked her what she meant.

"She told me it was because I relied on other people that I almost died in New Orleans. I was waiting on someone else to get me out of the pit I was in. She said I had been living that way since I left home.

"I asked her how she made enough to feed her kids and she showed me her garden and chickens. I was stunned, really. My folks never knew anything about chickens and our garden was just enough to keep Pop happy with fresh tomatoes in the summer.

"She had two full acres of beans and corn, with cabbages, carrots, onions, you name it. And she had close to forty chickens. She said she sold whatever they didn't need and canned a bunch for the winter. She sold her eggs to a man who took them to a farmers market to resell and paid her power bill from the sale of those eggs! She also sold chicks to those wanting to have chickens and took in laundry for some of the neighbors.

Kenny looked at Ted and smiled.

"Including that redneck. He is the reason her husband left and he also taught her how to live off of her wits and the land."

"How did you make her husband leave?" I asked Ted.

"I don't like bullies. I saw him knock her around one too many times, and I went over and had some words with him."

Kenny laughed. "Yeah, he went over to have words with a tire iron and .45. Tommy spent two weeks in the hospital."

"And you spent six months in jail," Anne said. "I remember that. They said you attacked him because you were upset to find out your neighbor was black."

"No, I never had a problem with blacks. I just had a problem with those who thought that being stronger meant you could do what you wanted."

"Yeah, well, Tommy kept beating on Sophia until he hears that Ted is getting out of jail. So he goes over to Ted's house and burns it down."

"What? When did he do that?" I asked.

"About two days before I got out of jail. They released me, I got some money from an ATM, hired a cab and got out to my place and it was burned to the foundation."

"What did you do?" At this point I was completely captured by his story.

"I found a poker from my fireplace in the ashes. I went over to Tommy's and knocked on the door. He opened it and laughed at me. Told me I was a stupid inbred cracker to think I could mess him up and not pay for it.

"I asked him if he had beaten his wife again. He told me it was none of my business. So I kicked the door open and walked in. He had a gun in his waistband, but I swung the poker until my arm was tired. His hand never found his gun. It slid across the floor. I got some newspaper and a metal pot from their kitchen and made myself a little fire-pit there in the living room. I set the end of the poker over the flames and told him I was going to get the poker red hot and then brand the words "wife beater" into his forehead. That is, unless he left the house that night."

"I take it he left that night?" I asked.

"Broken wrist, missing tooth, and jacked up eye. He grabbed whatever he could of value and left in their car. Sophia was furious. She was screaming at me, saying she and her kids were going to starve. I went back to my place and slept in the woods. The next day I started building a shelter and set snares for rabbits.

"Sophia came over and watched me for an hour and left. She did that a couple of times before she asked me what I thought I was doing. I told her I was rebuilding and going to live off the land. Eventually, I taught her to do the same. She had it all going when this guy showed up."

Kenny laughed. "Yeah, when I saw my sis was making it even though she was dirt poor, I thought she had been suckered into some scam by this redneck. So I went over and looked at his place and realized he was about as broke as she was. They were doing what I never realized I had always wanted to do."

"What was that?" I asked.

Kenny pointed to the U.S. flag flying in the town square. "Live without relying on anyone else. The American dream."

I was shocked we were already back in town. The saddle had been heavy, but the story these men told had kept me distracted from my discomfort. I set the saddle down and stretched. People were gathering around when I realized what made Ted a leader. He wasn't a follower.

NINE

"I'll take a look, but I don't know why Anne said I could fix it. I just tinkered with electronics when I was younger. I didn't go to school for it or anything," I said.

"It's not a high tech fix I'm looking for, David. I just need to see if we can figure a way to power up the receiver. I think if we can do that, we can get some news," Ted replied

"What news do you expect?"

"I don't know, but anything is better than nothing."

"Want to send Farrin out to Poplar Bluff? They might have a radio there."

"Not after what he found at Wilcox. If he was shot and chased driving up on a small town, I can't imagine what he might run into at a place like Poplar Bluff."

I nodded. The smoke from the west that morning a week ago made us all curious. We didn't know if it was a forest fire that might endanger us or maybe a controlled burn trying to signal for help. We sent Farrin and his motorcycle to find out. He returned an hour later. It took him a good hour and six beers to describe what he saw. The entire town of Wilcox looked like it was engulfed in flames. There were clumps of men roving the area, burning what they didn't want and taking what they did. Mostly women and whatever they could load into wagons.

One band of men saw him and called for him to stop. When he turned and drove off, he heard several gunshots. He never looked back.

It was decided then no one would go out to scout alone. Every road into Kenton was also watched by groups of armed men. Every day since, we had seen more and more fires pop up from the west. The bands of raiders and destroyers stayed away from Kenton. We assumed they had sent scouts as well, and had seen we were prepared to defend ourselves.

"We may need to send someone into Poplar Bluff eventually," Ted said. "We are running low on basic medicines. I don't know that we can legitimately trade for some from people there, but…"

"There might be some in medicine cabinets that were left behind by their owners," I finished for him.

"You don't like that, do you David?"

I shook my head. "No, makes me feel like we are not better than Lester and his group."

"Well we are, we just need medicine. Going through people's houses might be distasteful, but that is what we are faced with.

"I agree, I just don't like it."

I picked up the radio and put it in my satchel. "Who told you to let me take a look at this thing?"

"Anne. When she heard you were able to fix the tractor and the well pump, she remembered you had a knack for putting things together when you were a kid."

"Those were mechanical in nature, this is electric. But I will see what I can do."

"No harm in trying, it's not like we are going to get less reception from it."

I smiled and slung my satchel over my shoulder. Clyde was needed to help move some trees today, so I would have to walk the four miles home from the library. The day of the event, the walk into town had made me tired. Now I could walk four miles without paying attention.

The days had turned warmer and the rains had come to a stop. The fields were planted with the food that would allow us to survive, and everyone anxiously awaited the first harvest of lettuce and beans. Anything other than radish and turnip soup seasoned with a little green onion and boiled squirrel.

I walked past one of the fields and waved at the boys in the field. Two of them carried rifles and several others had sharp spades. Those with the rifles were scanning the edges of the field making sure no rabbits came in to eat the precious crops. Those with spades walked along each row, making sure no moles or other burrowing varmint was making itself at home.

The boys waved back and went back to their vigilant sentry work.

I shook my head as I thought about what Lexi would say if she had seen this. She was afraid of guns. She never grew up around them and did not like them. I didn't care one way or another. To me, they were just another tool. One I grew up with, but found no particular joy in using. It was like a hammer. Lexi was afraid of them and didn't want one in the house, so I acquiesced to her demand.

But now they were needful things. The right tool for the right job. At night, the dogs were set free in the field and the snares were set along the edges. But in the daytime, a stray rabbit taken with a .22 meant not only saving our crops, but more meat in our stew.

I dreamed about Lexi and Emma often, but each day I felt further from them. I didn't know if they were okay, or even alive. I pushed that thought out of my mind. I would just have to find them. Eventually. Some how.

Noon was approaching and that meant Mom would be cooking. She always found something to cook. Recently it's been dandelion greens with a little oil and salt. Not much of a lunch, but it fills the belly and it's as bad as I would have imagined.

The soybean fields across the road were full of green, but there wasn't much in the way of a meal from that. Some people suggested we could harvest the crop when ready and process oil from the beans and trade it to other towns. I didn't think there was much chance of us finding people who would want to trade anything useful for some cooking oil. But who knows. It would give us something to do and we would have plenty of cooking oil for ourselves, in any case.

As my parent's house came into view, I saw my dad washing my car. I blinked a couple of times and then looked back. He was washing my car. I approached the driveway and walked up behind him. He was on his knees with a soapy wet rag washing one of the tires.

"Taking her out for a spin?" I asked.

Dad turned and smiled at me. "No, just had some leftover water from laundry and didn't want to just dump it in the ditch.

I nodded. Soapy water was dumped in the ditch, cooking water was saved for the fields.

"So, you figured you would make sure my car was the best looking one on the street?"

"I would have washed mine, but you're blocking me in the garage," he said.

He started to stand and I reached over and took his arm. He nodded and smiled as I helped him to his feet.

"You finally convinced your mom I shouldn't be on the digging crews, and for some reason that's one of the things she won't forget. So I'm stuck at home helping her clean. You would be amazed at how boring retirement is when you can't watch television."

"Or dig latrines."

"Or dig latrines," he repeated. "What's in the satchel?"

"A radio. Anne told Ted to let me take a look at it. Don't know what I can do."

Dad picked up the bucket of water and carried it toward the ditch. "You were always taking apart my stuff when you were a kid. Always wanted to know how it worked."

"I always got it back together."

"Except the remote."

"Oh yeah," I said. "Except the remote."

"Maybe you can see what is busted and figure a way to fix it," Dad said.

"I just don't want to feel like I'm not doing work on one of the digging crews or working the field."

Dad dumped the bucket and looked back at me. "Now you know how I feel."

I walked back into the garage with him.

"Nice job on the car, by the way," I said. "You did that with just a rag and that bucket of dirty laundry water?"

"That's how we used to have to wash cars. You remember, that's how we washed cars together when you was a kid."

"I remember. Just seems so long ago."

"Looks like your mom has lunch ready," Dad said as we went in the kitchen.

He was right. Mom had set out two bowls of soup. She looked at me with surprise.

"David, I'm sorry. I didn't know you were going to be home for lunch."

"That's okay, Mom. I didn't tell you."

"Let me get another bowl and I'll split some of this up. I just wish we had some crackers left."

"No, Mom. I'm fine. I had something to eat in town. You two enjoy lunch, I'm going to go work on the radio."

I wasn't sure Mom bought the story that I wasn't hungry, but she made no more mention of dividing their meager meal with me. I wasn't all that hungry, anyway. I was more concerned about opening the radio and seeing if I could somehow figure out what was damaged and worried if I could figure out how to fix it.

I put my satchel on the bed and took out the case containing the radio. Ted had given me a pack of four AA batteries the radio could run on if needed. I set them aside on the end table by the bed and opened the case itself.

It was smaller than I imagined. It had an attachable hand microphone, like an old CB from the trucker movies I watched growing up. It also had a hand crank to provide a charge in case the batteries were dead. I took the radio over to the desk I had cleared off that morning in preparation.

That looked like a good place to start, so I turned the crank. Nothing. No indication the crank did anything. I pulled out the small tool kit I had in the second desk drawer since I was ten or so and started dissembling the complicated device.

Wilson Harp   EMP

I had been working on it for at least an hour when I heard shouting coming from the kitchen. I stopped and listened.

Mom was screaming and swearing at Dad for some reason. I couldn't understand Dad's replies, but it sounded like he was trying to calm her down. She was angry because the refrigerator was broken and he had been promising all week to get Sears to come and deliver a new one.

I sighed as I tried to focus on the radio again. I still had no idea what was wrong with it, but I did have most of it pulled apart correctly. One small plastic tab had snapped off, but that was typical when messing with electronics like this. I pulled out a plastic bag from the desk and selected several bundles of copper wire. I had found them while going through Dad's toolshed and thought they might come in handy at some point. They likely were from when I was a kid and played with electronics.

A few of the components of the radio had a strong odor, like burnt plastic. I figured those were probably the parts that had been damaged during the EMP. I set those aside and tried to figure out what I could do with the rest.

"David!"

I jumped out of the chair and was at the door to my room before I realized it. My name had been shrieked by Mom and it was full of panic and fear.

I threw the door open and was down the hall in three quick steps.

"Pat? Pat! David! Wake up Pat!"

Mom was in the garage. I raced through the kitchen and saw Mom kneeling over Dad as he lay on the garage floor beside their car.

Tears were streaming down Mom's cheeks. Dad's eyes opened and he blinked a few times. His right hand raised and then fell back down.

I hurried down the few steps and moved behind Mom.

"I'm here. Did he fall?" I asked.

"Oh David, he's awake. He's awake."

"Did he fall, Mom? Did he hit his head?"

"I don't know. I don't think so."

"Help me up," Dad said. His arms started moving and his eyes opened. He shut them again and exhaled deeply. "To the sofa. Get me to the sofa."

I reached down and tried to pull him up, but he was dead weight. I was able to get a good grip under his arms and was able to lift him most of the way up.

"Grab his legs," I told Mom.

She nodded and picked up his legs.

"Good," Dad said. "I don't think I wanted to lay there anymore."

I worked my way up the three steps into the kitchen. Once my feet hit the worn linoleum, I slowed to give Mom time to navigate the steps. We carried Dad into the living room and laid him on the sofa.

"Go get him some water, David," Mom said as she kneeled by Dad's head.

I went to the kitchen and poured some water from the large pitcher into a glass. Mom and Dad spoke to each other, but I couldn't hear what they were saying.

I brought the glass to Mom and handed it to her.

"On our dresser is a medicine bottle. Get a pill out of that and then go and get a baby aspirin from the medicine cabinet," Mom said.

I nodded and went back to their bedroom. I was amazed Mom was so clear and determined. The adrenalin of seeing Dad on the ground must have sharpened her attention and focus.

I found the bottle on the well-organized dresser and opened it. As I shook out one of the pills, I realized Ted was right. Billy had already told me he would only have enough pills for Mom for another few months and none for Dad at all.

Dad would need to really watch his stress level and not exert himself. We also needed to find more meds for him, and that likely meant rooting through the possessions of people who no longer needed them. Stealing from the dead was not how I wanted to survive.

I got the aspirin from the medicine cabinet in their bathroom and went back to where Dad was laying. He was propped up a bit and watched me as I came out of the hallway over to the sofa.

"Sorry about that, Davey," he said. "I guess I lost my balance."

"You had a heart attack, Dad," I said as I gave him the pills.

"No," said Mom. "It wasn't a heart attack. If it was, we would need to call an ambulance and we can't do that."

"It was a heart attack, Abbey," Dad said. "And we can't call an ambulance. We'll just have to make do with what we have."

Mom's eyes swelled with tears. She had been crying before, but now the tears flowed like little streams. They dripped off her chin as she sobbed.

"Don't you say that Pat. Don't you say that. We have to find a way."

My jaw slid open as I didn't know any words to comfort her. I looked at Dad and he waved me away. His arms pulled Mom close to him and he mouthed "it's okay" to me.

I didn't feel right leaving them when he was so weak and Mom was in tears, but I retreated to my old room. I closed the door behind me and leaned against it. Thoughts of losing one or both of my parents overwhelmed me and I began to cry. Then thoughts of Emma and Lexi came into my head. Had I already lost them? What possible way could I reach them? Could I ever know what happened?

I found myself laying on my bed, sobbing into my pillow. I had pushed my wife and daughter out of my mind as much as I could. I pretended it was because I had so many other pressing issues. But I didn't want to deal with the thought that, as bad as things were in Kenton, they were likely ten times as bad in Oak Park.

We had every modern convenience there, and that meant nothing after the EMP hit. There was no farm lands. There were no survivalists like Ted and Kenny. There weren't even people like Lester.

I prayed then. I hadn't prayed that hard in years. I prayed that the EMP would never have happened. That I would wake and discover it had been a very long, very real dream.

Then I prayed Lexi and Emma were safe. That they were somehow making their way down here. Or I could make my way up there.

Then I prayed I could just get some news of them. That I could talk to them and tell them I was okay. Find that they were okay. Find a way to let them know I loved them.

As I prayed this last bit, my head turned and I looked at the dissembled radio on the desk.

If I could fix the radio, I could find someone near Chicago who could let me speak to my daughter and my wife. If I could fix the radio, Luke Carter could speak to his wife in Houston.

That's why the radio was so important. That's why Anne had told Ted I could fix it.

Because I had to.

TEN

The sweat made my t-shirt stick to my back as I knelt in the row of beets. Today was the first day of harvesting a new crop. I never cared for beets, but anything that would add a different flavor to the soups and stews we were eating would be a blessing.

"How are you doing, Kenny?" I asked.

Kenny looked up from his side of the row. "I don't mind working to harvest crops, I just wish it was a little better than beets I was digging up."

"Soon we will be eating better," I said. "Just a few more weeks."

I looked over at the wheat and corn fields. It would be a month before those would even start to produce even the smallest of kernels, but I knew many people, like myself, stared at the knee-high fields and imagined what it would be like to have some bread or corn.

I stood up and my t-shirt was caught in a stray breeze. It pulled the fabric away from my skin and gave me a blast of what almost felt like an air conditioner. It was my Dad's shirt and six weeks earlier, it wouldn't have fit me. My stomach and arms would have been too pudgy to be enclosed in his smaller clothes.

Now the shirt flapped in the breeze. I would have hoped for more muscle, but a growling stomach was part of my day. Malnutrition had been kept at bay thanks to the Hansons and their pharmacy. They doled out vitamins where they could and treated the worst cases of intestinal ailments from a closely guarded stock of medicine.

Sharon Little had also been a source of great help when it came to keeping people healthy. That wasn't completely true. Her books on natural living had some valuable information about how to make home remedies for various sickness and conditions, but Sharon herself had been a pain in the ass to anyone she spoke to.

The instructions on the use of plants to create teas and tinctures were very helpful though. Sharon's young sons were pleasant children who did their best to help, so most people held their tongue about her complaints and unreasonable demands.

I looked at the bucket at my feet and realized I still needed another half row of beets before I was done filling it. The greens would be washed and lightly steamed. The beets themselves would be stewed and cleaned and added to the soups for the evening meal.

The sound of a horse whinny drew my attention and I looked to see Clyde and four men with shovels walking along the edge of the field toward the knot of evergreen trees. Beyond that was the communal burial spot. The trailer the horse was pulling had three sheet-wrapped bodies. One about five feet long and then two smaller ones.

"Luke," I called to the men attending the sad procession.

Luke Carter waved back at me and signaled me to come over.

I put down the bucket of beets and joined the group of men. I heard Kenny behind me and slowed so he could catch up.

"Three at once?" I asked as we drew near. The town was losing eight to ten people a day. Starvation, exhaustion, and weariness was taking its gruesome toll. Occasionally we would find a couple of dead in a single house in the morning, but most families and houses had not been touched.

"Sharon Little and her sons," Luke said.

I shook my head as if I hadn't heard him correctly.

"I… I just saw her and the boys yesterday. They all looked in good health."

"Someone gave Tyler a bit of roasted squirrel. He liked it," Luke said. "It's in her note."

A note. That means it was a suicide.

"And she took her boys with her?" I asked.

Luke nodded. "She did. She didn't want her boys to be polluted with our world. I guess if she couldn't keep them from the impure foods and animal flesh we were polluting ourselves with, she wanted them dead."

"Dear God."

"Yeah, we sent the letter on to Ted. He and the council might be able to figure out a bit more. A bad situation."

I walked with the men a few more minutes. I didn't look at the wrapped bodies. I couldn't after knowing who they were.

"I better get back to the beet field. We're taking every fifth one today," I said.

"Good," said Luke. "Beets will be a good addition. You know the Ellison's left this morning, don't you?"

"I saw the car heading out. I can't believe Ted let them take it."

"There was some loud talk with him, I was there," Kenny said

Luke shrugged. "In the end, it wasn't Ted or the council's decision to make. He knows it is dangerous, but they have family in Little Rock and with Barb dying last week… well, without his mom around anymore, I guess he figured he would try to get back home and see what it is like down there."

"Maybe we will get word from him one day," I said.

"Maybe. If you can get that radio up for more than a minute at a time, we can try to give him a call."

"I'm working on it, Luke," I said. I got the radio activated, but it kept losing power for some reason after a few seconds. There was only static in those moments, so I wasn't even sure if the receiver was working. Just static in the speaker. But it was a start.

"I know you are, David. I just want to be there when we hear news of the outside world."

"You will be, Luke. Well, I really do need to get back to digging these beets up. We will be starting on some of the green beans next week, they say."

"Looking forward to it. You take care, David, and tell your folks I'll stop by tonight."

"Hey David, I'm going to go into town now, can you take my bucket in?" Kenny asked.

"Sure, will you be back tomorrow?"

"I will, unless something comes up."

I gave Kenny a wave and watched as he turned toward town. He filled in wherever there was work to be done, but lately he had taken to working in the fields with me. I asked him about that and he just responded he liked talking to me.

I walked back to the beets and picked up Kenny's bucket. I carried it over to where I had left mine and emptied Kenny's beets into what I had gathered and then set back to digging. After twenty minutes I had the third bucket of the day done.

I picked up my bucket, slid it into Kenny's empty bucket, and headed toward the Marsh's house where the women of the area were gathered in a small camp.

I don't think there was a specific day when it was decided cooking communally was the best way to feed people. It just happened, and within a few days there were little knots of women cooking and tending to the laundry on Millie Marsh's front yard. Clothes had to be washed by hand and mended with needle and thread and that work seemed to go smoother when there was talk.

I wondered how Lexi was dealing with this new world. She was a feminist to her core. Although I think it had more to do with not wanting to do dishes than any aspect of equality. She would not have been one of the women who dug latrines or graves. She would not have been with the hunters or the teams who cut wood. She might have been in the fields tending the crops, but I bet she would have fit in best with the women sewing, cooking and washing. They were the happiest people in the town. At least they laughed the most.

The women in the small camp in front of the Marsh's house were subdued when I arrived. The edges of whispers I could hear were about Sharon Little and her boys. Mostly about her boys.

There were a few women talking about the Ellison's and what they hoped they would find when they got home. Some were convinced the people down in Little Rock were doing just as well, if not better, than us in Kenton. Others argued Kenton had its head together and other places were likely falling apart. A good many of those believed we would see the Ellison's car back in town before too much longer.

I grimaced as I thought about the loss of the car. It was a 1961 Oldsmobile. It had originally belonged to Jerry Ellison. His widow, Barb, only drove it around town since his death. I was still in high school at that time. It was one of only three cars that still worked in town and was, by far, the most dependable and biggest.

But Bill Ellison had two daughters in college back in Little Rock, so he loaded up his wife and two teenage girls and set off to see if he could reunite his family.

Maybe the grimace wasn't so much over the loss of the car as it was jealousy of what he might be able to accomplish. I set the bucket of beets down by Millie Marsh.

"That's one out of five in the first two rows," I said.

She looked at them and waved over a teenage girl. It was Sarah Johnson. She had changed so much since I had seen her the night of the EMP, I didn't recognize her at first.

Millie took out about a third of the beets from the bucket and set them on a large towel on a low bench.

"Take this bucket up to the Davidson's and Leferney's. Split it evenly between the two," she said to Sarah.

"Is there anything I can do to help?" I asked.

"Take a seat and a knife. Cut off the tops of the beets and put the greens in this bowl," she said.

I smiled and took a knife that was sitting on a nearby table. I then dropped next to the beets and started doing as I was told. That was the best way of dealing with Millie Marsh. Do what you were told.

I cut the tops off of the beets and then took the bowl of greens over to a woman who was cutting up radishes and onions. She had already blanched a large pile of dandelion greens, so I figured she was the one who would portion out our salad that night.

She took the bowl with a nod and went back to chatting with the woman on her other side. I didn't know her name. Even after a month of seeing her several times, I had no idea who she was or what her story was like. I didn't want to know.

Over three hundred people had died in Kenton. Many more would die in the upcoming months. The heat, the malnutrition, maybe even an outbreak of a disease would take many. I didn't want to know each name. I didn't want to know each story. I'd leave that to Luke Carter.

I went back to Millie and sat down on the grass. I was tired. Bone tired as my dad would say. I would wait until the meal was ready and take it home, just over a mile, eat it and then go work on the radio until the sun went down.

Then I would lay on the bed and pray for rain, pray for safety for Lexi and Emma, and pray for my parents. I generally would fall asleep sometime in that routine. Then I would wake up with a start and begin another day of just trying to survive.

"David," said Millie. "Go get your container, we are about ready to serve up the stew. Had four rabbits and two ducks brought in today, so you all will get a few bites of meat."

"What about the beets?" I asked. She was washing them carefully in a tub of water.

"Tomorrow. We'll stew them separate and add them as a side."

I was looking forward to having a bit more variety in the stew, but with rabbit and duck meat tonight, it should be a filling dinner. I looked at the field with the wheat growing and felt my mouth get moist thinking about a piece of bread to go with dinner.

I went and gathered the container I would bring back, washed and dried, the next morning. I handed it to Millie and she ladled four large spoonfuls of stew. I noted she went out of her way to add some extra meat to the container.

"You make sure your dad gets some of that rabbit," she said. "He needs to keep his strength up."

"I will, Millie. I'll be here tomorrow to get you some more beets," I said as I took the container of hot stew. I went to where the greens were being prepared and collected the small bag that contained our side.

It was amazing how much just a few bites of vegetables could satisfy the growling stomach. My thoughts drifted to what I would normally eat on a salad. I'd have carrots and cucumbers, tomatoes and croutons. Oh, croutons! Those would be missing for quite some time. At least the carrots, cucumbers and tomatoes would be available in the next month or so.

We just had to make it through this week, and then maybe the next, but more varieties of crops would come in. Once we made it through the summer, we would have the fall harvest to look forward to. Pecans and walnuts, apples and peaches. I had heard there were some berries that would be available in the summer, but I really didn't know about any berries except strawberries. And the farmers agreed they weren't worth the effort. We needed foods that could be keep us going, not just foods that would be flavorful.

I knew thinking about different foods wouldn't help my stomach pangs or help me focus on what I needed to think on. I looked around and saw I was already halfway home. My pace increased as I thought about working on the radio. Maybe I was putting too much power through it? Maybe I had missed a critical area? What about the capacitors? Could one of those have burned out?

I had been over all of those questions before and hadn't been able to figure it out, but I was sure I was close to the solution.

Mom was out front of the house with a bucket and a pile of clothes when I approached. She waved at me and went back to her work. I had suggested to dad she go and work for Millie, but he didn't like that idea. She had been pretty good these last couple of weeks, but he was worried what would happen if she had a bad day. The worst she could do here is break our stuff, ruin our water, or knock over our outhouse, again.

There, he said, she could ruin food for fifteen families in one outburst.

I agreed, grudgingly.

"David," Mom said as I drew near. "Did you hear the news?"

"No, Mom. What news?"

I leaned down and kissed her on the cheek.

She kissed me back and smiled.

"They found some deer!" she said. Her eyes twinkled. She looked ten years younger when she was happy and I could tell she was focused and clear.

"That's great," I said. "Who got it?"

"Three. Buck and his boys got three. Two does and a buck. Buck got the buck." She laughed. "Isn't that funny?"

"Sure is," I said with a laugh. "Where are they?"

"Hanging out in front of Buck's garage, from what I understand."

"When will they butcher them?"

"I'm not sure. Your dad went down there to see."

"Okay, I'm going to go put our stew in the house and wash up for supper."

"Thank you, David," Mom said as she went back to her work.

I went through the garage and into the kitchen. I set the container of stew on the counter and the bag of salad on the table.

I didn't remember the last time I had been alone in the house. It was an odd feeling, one I did not enjoy.

I walked back to my room. I intended to look at the radio for a few minutes before supper, but instead I turned and looked into my parent's bedroom. It was essentially the same as when I grew up. The bed and dressers were the same and in the same location. The curtains on the window were the same ones my mom had hung when I was a child. They were a gift from Aunt Alice.

This room was a place of shelter. A solid point in the chaos of life. No matter what was going on in my life, I could know this room would always be here and always be the same.

I thought about Emma. What had I established that had given her a point of solidity to hold onto? We had moved often as both Lexi and I advanced in our careers. We changed furniture on a whim, the layout of rooms without consideration. The only unchanging element for Emma was we were together as a family. And now we weren't.

"Davey?"

"Here, Dad," I answered.

I walked back into the kitchen. Dad had opened the container with the stew and was looking at it.

"No beets?" he asked.

"Missus Marsh said they would add them tomorrow."

He looked up as he did when he was considering what to say.

"She's getting food stored up. That's more clever of her than I would have thought. Maybe the council had that idea," he said after a few seconds.

"Stored up?"

"We have been living day to day, Davey. And while that is no small feat, we need to start storing some food for a rainy day."

"I think that phrase is more literal now," I said.

"Indeed." He closed the container and motioned me to sit down. "Did you hear about the deer?"

I nodded as I sat down. "I understand they took three."

"Yes, and Buck says he saw at least four more."

"Sounds like the deer are coming closer to town again."

"It does. That's good news for us, as we will get more meat in our diet, but it also means the coyotes might be heading back in as well."

"We'll have to keep an eye on the kids and pets," I said.

"There is always a balance, you know? When something good happens, there is often a danger associated with it. And when something bad happens, there is often an opportunity."

Mom walked into the kitchen with her empty laundry basket.

"Oh, I hope I didn't interrupt anything serious," she said as she saw us at the table.

"No. Not at all dear," Dad said as he stood and took the laundry basket from her.

"You may want to check on those clothes in a bit," Mom said looking out at the laundry drying on the clothes line. "A storm's coming."

ELEVEN

I held Emma's hand as I helped her up the crumbling wall.

"Hurry," Lexi called. She was standing on the remains of the tower and waving us up.

I pulled Emma up the last few feet and she fell into me, giggling and smiling.

She was eight years old again. No, fourteen.

"Will you two hurry up?" Lexi asked. She laughed and we were standing with her.

I turned my head back and saw the land behind me burning. Desolation stretched as far as I could see.

"We're almost there Dave," Lexi said.

I turned to look at my wife and daughter. They stood on the tower and were looking out on the land we were struggling to reach.

I screamed as a bolt of lightning hit the tower.

Everything was dark, then the thunder hit and I tried to open my eyes.

"David?" Mom asked. "Are you alright?"

I shook my head and realized that my eyes were open, it was just pitch black in the room. It was a dream. I had dreamed of my wife and daughter again. I heard their voices, I felt their presence. But it was just vivid echoes of the dream.

"I'm okay, just a bad dream," I yelled back to Mom.

I lay back on the bed and was startled by a flash of light. The storm was here.

All through the evening before, we could see the line of clouds march from the West.

I had always mocked the weathermen on television. They didn't seem to know what was going to happen any more than the average person. Now I missed the general information they could provide.

Was the storm merely a line of thunder that would go past us overnight or would it be a system that would be with us for days? Would we have high winds, tornadoes or hail?

Of all of those, hail scared me the most. In the past, hail would have meant an irritating phone call to the insurance agent and a trip to the body shop. Maybe I would have to climb a ladder and check for damage to the roof.

Now, hail meant we could lose some of our crop. Losing our crop would mean starvation and more people in graves.

I grew restless as I considered what could happen, so I left the bed and went to the window. The storm silenced the normal sounds night brought to life and performed a symphony of its own. The sound of wind combined with the creaks, whistles, and thumping of the trees and buildings.

When illuminated by street lights and the ambient glow of modern life, the sounds were recognizable and ordinary. In the darkness that smothered the town tonight, however, it brought to mind all of the fears and terrors I had as a very young child.

We are all afraid of the dark to some extent. It's the fear of the unknown, and more, the fear we can't see something that might be able to see us.

Lightning slashed through the sky and I could see the Johnson's house clearly. Some animal was walking through the yard. I barely saw it. It may have been a cat, opossum, or even a skunk. The image was burned onto my eyes, but not clearly enough to be sure.

The thunder rolled in a few seconds later. I put on a pair of jeans and left my room. I could feel a strong draft of air coming down the hall and knew the front door stood open.

"Can't sleep?" I asked softly as I turned the corner.

I couldn't see him, but I knew Dad stood near the open doorway.

"Never could sleep through storms." Dad lied. He never woke, even in the worst storms, when I was young.

"Have the rains started yet?" I made my way through the living room to stand by the door.

"No, not yet. Should be soon. Smells like it is about to drop."

"Think it will hail?"

"Hope not," he said. "We sure don't need to lose the wheat."

We stood in silence as we waited for the rain to start.

"Do you dream about food, Davey?"

"Sometimes," I said. "Mostly I dream about Lexi and Emma. But I dream about food sometimes."

"I feel guilty about that, Davey. I asked you to make time to come down here. I thought you needed to spend time with your mom, and I needed something to take my mind off of things. I didn't mean for you to leave your family behind."

"It's not your fault, Dad. It's no one's fault. If things... if things were different, we might have all been down here together. But things are what they are."

The rain started to fall. It was a heavy rain that fell in solid sheets. It wasn't a gradual rain, it was one which starts like someone threw a switch. The smell of wet earth rushed into our open house. The rain brought the frigid air from the upper atmosphere with it and I shivered as the temperature dropped,

"What food do you dream about, Dad?"

"Sounds odd, but cookies mostly."

"Mom's snickerdoodles?"

Dad chuckled. "No, but don't tell her that. I dream about chocolate chips cookies for the most part. They have always been my favorite."

"Cookies do sound good. In fact, anything bread-like would be a dream."

"Well, when we get the wheat in, separated, and ground, I would get ready for basic, flat bread for a while."

"Flat bread?"

"Not a lot of yeast, I'm figuring."

"What about sourdough?" I asked.

"Don't know. Maybe someone in town will know how to make bread from scratch. Maybe Sharon Little has a book that has that trick."

"Dad, Sharon took her life yesterday."

The sound of the rain filled the silence for a few minutes.

"What about her boys? Did she take them, too?"

"Yeah, she did."

Dad swore under his breath.

"I'll go over to her house and look for any books we can put to use tomorrow," he said.

"Some people just crack under this pressure, I suppose," I said.

"No. Cracking under the pressure is understandable. Giving up is unforgivable. She didn't need to take those boys with her. That shows her character more than anything else. She decided if life couldn't be lived on her terms, then it wasn't worth living for anyone."

"I just want to get through tomorrow. And the next day. And the next."

Dad put his hand on my arm. "Davey, I want you to get your family back. That is what I want. Me and your mom… we can do alright. If you think you can find a way to get back to Chicago, I think you should."

"Thanks, Dad. I just don't know how to even start. It's almost five hundred miles. I figure even if I can walk twenty miles a day, that is still almost a month. And I would need to make sure I had plenty of food and water."

"Well, figure a pound of food a day, and a quart of water. That's what? Eighty pounds of food and water for the trip?"

"I don't think I could make a trip with an eighty pound pack strapped to my back. And I would have to cross the Mississippi. I just don't know."

"Don't give up, Davey. And don't look at the problem. That will make you feel overwhelmed. Look for the solution, like you are with the radio."

"I don't know that I have a solution for the radio. Not yet anyway."

"Don't give up. If you are working on it, then likely there are others that are as well. If so, then we should be able to communicate with other towns when you get it working."

"What about you, Dad? What do you want? If I left, what would you have to keep you and Mom going?"

"I don't know. To eat a chocolate chip cookie," he laughed. "That would be a good start. I'd like the thrill of feeling the wind blow on my face while riding in a car. I'd like a reason to have to put on a suit again. I like my old suit, but I'm afraid it will hang in my closet until it rots."

He turned to me. "Say, not to be morbid, but when I pass, bury me in that suit."

"I really don't want to think about that, Dad," I whispered.

The rain had shifted to a steady shower while we had talked. The lightning and thunder didn't seem as close, but each time the sky lit up, we could see nothing but a solid roof of clouds.

"We probably shouldn't be standing in this doorway. Might catch a cold," I said.

"You go on back to bed. I'll stay up and watch the rain a bit more."

I pulled Dad in for a hug. He patted my shoulder and I made my way back to my room. This night was a reflection of our current situation. We knew things were happening outside of our ability to perceive them, but we would have to wait until the storm passed and the morning dawned in order to see what we had experienced.

I shut the door to my room and slid my jeans off. I sat on the edge of my bed and thought about what Dad said. Could I start the trip up to Chicago? What would I need to take with me? Could I go alone?

The bands of raiders that had burned and looted Wilcox were a major concern. If I left and was killed on the way, then I couldn't help Lexi and Emma, nor could I help Mom and Dad. I would just be dead.

I felt guilty as I thought that. It felt like I was justifying my cowardice. I suppose I was, to a certain point. But the reality was, I could do something useful here. I could fix the radio and get us in contact with others who were keeping their towns together.

Once we had a way to talk to others, I could figure a way to get to Chicago and start looking for my family.

Lighting lit my room again, and I yawned. I was too tired to work on the radio, anyway, so I decided to get some sleep. I lay down and soon I was dreaming of Emma and chocolate chip cookies at a birthday party.

The next morning I woke and looked at the window. Sunshine should have pushed me awake some time before. I pulled my pocket watch from the nightstand and looked at it. Nine o'clock. This was the latest I had slept in a long time. Months, maybe a year.

I looked over at the window and saw the sky was dark and gray. I sat up, stretched my arms above my head and listened for a minute. The sound of rain was soft and steady, not like the wind-swept torrents when I stood at the door last night. I heard some movement in the kitchen, so I knew at least one of my parents was awake.

I grabbed my jeans and shoes and got dressed. I went into the kitchen where my Dad had a candle burning on the table. He was reading a book.

"Good morning, David," Mom said.

I turned and saw her working on a piece of cross-stitch she had found. She hadn't done cross-stitch since I was quite young.

"Morning Mom," I said.

"Take the umbrella," Dad said as I started to open the garage door. Just inside the garage was an open umbrella drying.

I never thought I would have to wear shoes and carry an umbrella just to pee in the morning, but here I was. Dad had hung two large, blue, plastic tarps over the entry to the garage the evening before, and it seemed to be effective. Even with the strong winds and heavy rains, the garage had remained dry.

I hopped and skipped across the muddy, puddle-riddled lawn back to where the outhouse was. Dad had built the privy in two days from scrap lumber and items in his work shed. It was well constructed. No rain had worked its way through the seams and joints of the small building. He had even brought out the seat from the main toilet and had installed the toilet paper holder.

Thanks to Mom being a little obsessive over having enough toilet paper 'in case company drops in', we still had an ample supply six weeks after our lives had shifted to this existence.

I had set the umbrella in the corner of the small enclosure and realized I had done the job the storm had failed to do; there was a small puddle of water in the outhouse. I mumbled about my own stupidity, picked up the umbrella and opened the door. I was about to step out when an odd sound caught my ear.

With the light rain and low wind, the morning was abnormally quiet. But I clearly heard a chain being moved next door at the Johnson's. I leaned out of the outhouse and looked at the neighbor's backyard. Bennie Johnson had a small shed he had bought for storage, and he had a light chain and padlock keeping it shut.

EMP   Wilson Harp

A man was pulling at the chain and had fit his arm inside the gap he had created.

"Hey," I said as I stepped out of the outhouse. "What do you think—"

The man darted away from the sound of my voice without looking toward me. He was ready to run at the first noise, and had shot out like a rabbit knowing there was a hawk in the air.

I stood stunned. I looked around, but he was gone and I had no idea who he was or where he could have run to. I went back into the garage, propped the umbrella up to dry and stepped into the kitchen.

"Shoes off," Dad said as I stepped in.

I kicked off my shoes and sat at the table.

"I think we should shut our garage door," I said. I spoke low so Mom wouldn't hear.

"Why?" asked Dad. He cut his eyes to me, but didn't move otherwise.

"I saw someone trying to break into the Johnson's shed as I was leaving the outhouse."

Dad nodded. "Someone tried to pry open the door to my shed. They also came through and took a couple of wrenches and screwdrivers from the garage the other day."

"Why didn't you tell me?"

"Everyone has enough to worry about. I figured it was some bored kid looking for a thrill. Not like he can sell the tools for money or anything."

"I don't like it, Dad. And this wasn't a kid. It was an adult."

Dad pushed himself back from the table and looked at me. "What did he look like?"

"Blue hoodie, jeans, medium build."

"See his face?"

"No."

"What shoes was he wearing?"

"Don't know, didn't pay attention."

"Okay. He sounds like he rattled you a bit. I'll see if we can file a report with Deputy McDaniels. Maybe he has some information and we can put a stop to this behavior."

I nodded. This had rattled me, but I wasn't sure why.

"I'll see if I can find him next time I go back into town," I said. "But it doesn't look like it will be today."

Dad shook his head. "No, I think this is one of those days where we should hunker down and eat a few cans out of the pantry."

"Really? What should we have?" Mom asked. She was on her feet and moving to the cabinet where we had the last of our long term food.

"I didn't think she was listening to us," I said.

"I did. If I hadn't told you to take your shoes off, I would have caught it later."

"What about some chicken noodle soup and for dessert some fruit cocktail?" Mom said, holding both cans out for our inspection.

"Sounds great, dear," Dad said. "I didn't think it was quite a fruit cocktail day, but now I see it, I can't think of a better thing to eat."

"I'm going to go read and see if I can figure out that radio," I said as I stood from the table. "When will we eat?"

"I think we can probably get the soup going soon and then we can save the fruit for later in the afternoon," Mom said. She was digging through her neglected cookware looking for the right pan. "Do we have any clean water to boil?"

"Not sure, Mom," I said. "Maybe you can just hold the pan out the front door and catch some rain."

Mom swatted at me with a ladle. "Don't be a smart aleck. Now, go get some water from the pump."

"Okay, Mom," I said as I bent and picked up my shoes. "But I expect to get a cherry in my portion of fruit cocktail for getting cold and wet for you."

I grabbed the water bucket and umbrella in the garage and headed out into the light rain. Sarah Johnson was at the well pumping water for her grandparents.

"Hi David," she said. "Rain is nice, huh?"

She was soaking wet and all smiles.

"No umbrella or jacket?"

"As hot as it's been, this is a nice change," she said. "There, pump's all yours."

"Thanks, Sarah."

She waved goodbye and headed back to her house.

I set the bucket under the spout and started pumping. Sarah was a couple of years younger than Emma and she had adjusted quite well to her situation. I remember the day she broke. Ted explained everyone would break at some point. He said once the normalcy bias had worn off and people accepted the new normal, there would be some trigger, some word, some event that would cause people to just break inside. It was the final step to the release of the previous existence and what would allow people to plan a future where they couldn't go back. Or even look back.

Sarah had broke when her grandmother's cat didn't come back home one night. She cried and bawled. Not for the cat, which she did care for, but for her parents and brothers. For her friends at school, her neighborhood, her house, her life. It was all gone and she realized there was nothing she could do to get them back. And there was nothing anyone else could do either.

Some people break and they can't deal with it. Hank Kroner was the first suicide and Sharon Little was the most recent, but over two hundred had taken their own lives in Kenton. Two hundred people had been broken and had not been able to see a way forward.

Sarah had cried for four days, even after the cat had returned. She went through the process of letting her past go and she now made each day better for herself and her grandparents. She would make it. She would push through.

I wondered if Lexi and Emma had broken yet. When they broke, would they be able to face it like Sarah?

I picked up the full bucket of water and started back to the house. The rain had picked up and I was soaking wet. I would need to dry off and change clothes before I found a book to read. I had to read. I had to escape. Because the truth was, I had not had my break yet.

TWELVE

The clouds thinned that night and the sun shone brightly the next morning. I was up early, before the first rays of light touched the muddy fields across the street, and went into the kitchen.

Dad had beaten me to the table, as usual, and was reading the book I had left out the night before.

"I never understood why you needed these books," he said. "But then, I wasn't much of a reader myself."

"What do you think?" I asked.

"Pretty interesting, once you get over the fact he isn't writing about things in our world."

"Hobbits and elves and stuff?"

"That, but I was referring more to the ideas of honor and chivalry and duty," Dad said. "This Tolkien guy really missed the world that had left him behind."

"That's true, he really did," I said as I poured a cup of water from the drinking pitcher.

"How is your stomach doing this morning?"

"Not bad," I said. "I woke up with some heartburn a couple of times."

"The sugar in the fruit cocktail," Dad said. "Didn't think about how much we had been away from that kind of food."

"I didn't realize how much I missed it. I would have thought after a while, it wouldn't have tasted as good as it did."

Dad turned a page in the book. "Food companies spent millions and billions of dollars on making us like their product so we would keep buying it."

"True. I do miss Oreos."

Dad smiled. "Everyone will dream of cookies."

"Until cookies are just a distant memory."

"I suppose so."

"Are you going into town today?"

"Probably. I want to check on the beet field first, but if it is too wet to harvest them, I plan on going into town to see if anyone brought in any old radios."

"When you do, look for Deputy McDaniels and report our prowler. I think I saw him near the Johnson's again last night."

"Okay. I'll let him know what is going on."

I prepared for the day and left the house. I walked out to the street and looked across the soybean field toward where the beets were planted. I felt lightheaded and terrified as I saw the wheat field just beyond the beets and onions.

All of the tall, green stalks looked like they were lying on the ground. Several men were walking the edges of the area. Sometimes they spoke with each other, sometimes they bent down as if to examine the fallen plants. I glanced over at the corn field and released a deep breath. The corn was standing straight and tall in their appointed rows.

I hurried over across the soybean field. I was careful not to step on any plants and to make sure I didn't slip and fall. When I reached the men, I could hear laughter of all things.

"David," Luke said as I approached. "You look upset. Is everything alright?"

"I don't know," I said as I looked at the flattened field of wheat. "Did we just lose our wheat crop?"

Several of the men chuckled and one came over and slapped me on the shoulder. It was Nate Milton. He had the biggest vegetable garden in town before this happened and had been a farmer all of his eighty years.

"No son," he said. His teeth looked rotten as he grinned at me. "The wheat just likes to lay down when it gets this wet. It will perk up again after a day or two in the sun."

I smiled and looked over the field. None of the stalks seemed damaged and they all looked to be pressed down in a uniform manner.

"Good," I said. "Good."

"Glad you approve, David," Luke said. "I guess I best be getting my work done for the day. And don't feel bad, I came running across the field same as you when I saw the condition of the wheat. I thought we were going to be without bread for the whole summer."

I smiled at Luke as he walked by me, but my eyes remained focused on the wheat. This close I could see the stalks were bent, not broken. And if Milton said they would be okay after a little sun, then that was good enough for me.

I left the wheat field and made my way over to the Marsh's house. Millie was waiting for me with a bucket.

"Need four buckets of beets today, David," she said. "I reckon most of the folks dug into their pantries a bit yesterday, but we have a few folks who are awfully hungry today."

I saw there was a good sized coal pit with several big slabs of river rocks directly on the smoldering wood. There were more than a few aluminum foil packages sitting on top of the stones.

"Roasting the beets?" I asked as I picked up the bucket.

"Yep, some folks like beets in their stew, some don't. Figured if we roasted them, then people could eat them as they like them."

I nodded and went to the field and knelt with the small trowel Millie had placed in the bucket. The rain had muddied the field, but it wasn't as easy to dig out the beets as I hoped it would be. The new growth of small white roots grabbed at the soaked soil.

It was probably ten o'clock by the time I filled the bucket. I wished I had carried my watch with me, but with as filthy as I had become, it was good I had developed the habit of leaving it on my desk.

I stood and carried the bucket over to Millie. She was in conference with several of the other women who had taken on the job of preparing the communal meals in their neighborhoods. They shared recipes, plans for what to serve, and trades for different foods.

Our area grew beets and onions, but not radishes or cabbage. Everybody grew wheat and corn, though. That was decided early on. The risk of a single fire or flooded field was too great to risk what would have to get us through the upcoming winter.

Millie saw me approach and made eye contact with me.

"Missus Marsh, I need to head into town. I'll be back to get more beets in a couple of hours," I said.

"Thank you, David," She said. "I'll get someone to help you today. Seems our beets are in demand."

She smiled as she went back to her conversation.

I left the gathering of white haired women positive I never wanted to negotiate for anything serious with any of them. Especially Millie.

I headed up to Granger Street and turned toward town. As I headed north along the road, I made sure I looked down the drive of Buck Fredrickson. His house set back a ways and was screened by a row of low poplar trees.

There were a few men working around his garage as I passed. They were butchering the three deer he had taken and it looked like they were ready to tan the deer hides. I wondered if that was something some of these men knew from before, or if it was something they were practicing for the first time.

When this started, I would have guessed Ted might know how to skin a deer and tan its hide into leather, but now I'm sure he would have just read about it and would be willing to try with no hesitation. It was amazing how much he knew and yet how much there was still to know. It was also surprising the types of things other people knew how to do. Anne could tan that hide, of that I was certain. Sue Hanson knew how to set rabbit and squirrel snares. I would have never guessed she and her sisters made money back in high school by trapping foxes and selling their furs.

"Need a bath, David?" Ted said as I approached the steps of the library.

I looked down at my clothes and realized I was caked in mud.

"I guess so," I said. "I was digging beets this morning."

"Well don't go tracking that in the library. What can I help you with?"

"Taking a break from the fields. Came in to see if anyone dropped off any electronics."

Ted shook his head. "Not today, sorry."

"Have you seen Deputy McDaniels?"

Ted looked around and shook his head. "No, he, uh…" He trotted down the last couple of steps to stand close to me. "He's been at Lester's more and more recently. I'm pretty sure he is sleeping there some nights. Maybe most by now."

I was stunned. Deputy McDaniels sure didn't like Ted and he really did not like Lester Collins. When Ted announced the deal Lester put forward, McDaniels protested in the strongest terms. He even accused Ted of setting up the deal himself and claimed Lester and Ted were working together.

If Anne hadn't been there to confirm the story, I suspected Ted might have been arrested.

Of course, there was no jail in Kenton. There was no police force either. The country sheriff handled all of our law enforcement issues and they were based in Wilcox. Our good deputy was the only sort of law man around.

And now he was up at the party camp.

"Do you know if he will be in today?" I asked.

"He has been crawling in here around noon or so. I didn't come down from my place yesterday, so I don't know if he was here. I haven't seen him yet this morning."

"Okay," I said. "I don't want to make a mess in the library. Could you get me a sheet of paper and a pen? I need to file a report with him."

"Sure," Ted said. He climbed the stairs and went in the library.

I leaned back on the bike rack and rolled my neck.

"Hey, David."

Deputy McDaniels turned the corner of the Library and started toward the steps.

"Hey Gary," I said.

He reeked of booze and pot. His uniform was unwashed and it looked like he had slept in it for weeks. He likely had. Mayor Mueller said when he was at the deputy's place, he noticed there were three other uniforms hung neatly in the closet. I noticed he wore his service belt, but his handgun was not in his holster.

The deputy started to amble past me.

"Gary," I said. "I need to report something."

He swayed some as he looked back at me. His eyes weren't focused and his posture indicated some unease with his balance. Hung-over or already stoned I assumed.

"What you got for me, Hartman?" he asked.

"We've had a problem with someone getting into our garage and our shed. In fact, a few folks down that way have had problems."

"You see anyone?"

"Yesterday morning, saw someone try to get into the Johnson's shed. When I shouted, he took off."

"Know who it was?" McDaniels asked. A small smile had crept onto his face.

"No, didn't get a good look."

"You don't know who it is, but you want me to do something about it. Is that what you want?"

"No, I just wanted to report it."

"Of course. I'll just get right on that. Someone breaking into your stupid garage. Yeah, that's what I'll concern myself with," he said. The sneer on his face and the anger in his voice caused me to step back.

"Here's the paper and pen, David," Ted said as he came out the door of the library. "Do you still need them?" He asked as he joined McDaniels and me at the bottom of the steps.

"No, I don't think so, Ted," I said. "I have already given the message to Gary."

"If you're looking for who might be breaking into places, you might want to check with Ted here, or his friend Kenny. Wouldn't surprise me at all," McDaniels said. "They know where everyone lives. They know what everyone has. And they still keep their own people away from town like we are infected with something."

"Deputy," Ted said. "Why don't you go in and see the mayor. He might have something to tell you."

"What would he have to tell me?" McDaniels asked.

"Just tell him Ted said he had a message. It's the proposal the council had a couple of days ago."

"One day, Riggins, me and you are going to have some words. And I don't think you're going to like what I have to say."

"One day I'm sure that will happen, Gary. But it won't be today. I have too much work to do today."

Deputy McDaniels spit on the ground and stalked up the steps to the library. Ted didn't take his eyes off of the law man until the front door of the building slammed shut.

"You should probably get going, David," said Ted. "Gary is going to be furious when he comes out in a bit.

He will likely be looking for someone to blame it on. I'm going to make myself scarce as well."

"What is the message?"

"Up until now, McDaniels hasn't found himself on any work schedules because he is our law man. But he hasn't been living up to that duty, so the council voted to have his exception revoked."

"You think he might become violent?" I asked.

"Maybe, but at least he left his sidearm up at Lester's. That was probably Lester's doing. I'll have to thank him for that the next time I see him."

"You see him a lot?"

"Every couple of days."

"Why?"

"Lester has come around a bit. I think he is realizing that death is not just lurking around the corner. As bad as this all is, I think he believed it would be much worse."

"How much worse?"

"Wilcox. The burning and looting that Farrin saw there. Kenton has held it together and we are starting to really gel as a community. I admit, there were a few days when I thought about heading west with Kenny, Sophia, her kids, and the others up at my place. Maybe we could find an Amish or Mennonite community to settle in with."

"I never thought about the Amish. They are probably doing pretty well."

Ted shrugged. "I'm sure it's affected them in some manner, but their day to day living has likely been close to the same as before."

"How are the people at your place doing?"

"Pretty good. Sophia has some strawberries coming in and the kids sure love that. I don't tell many people all we have up there, because... you know."

I knew. Too many people would see that as unfair somehow. They wouldn't care about the fact Sophia, Ted and the others had been growing their own food up there for years. They wouldn't care with Ted and Kenny doing so much work in town, those who stayed up there would have extra work to do. Many people would just want some for themselves. And that would be trouble.

"There are some blackberry bushes and I think some huckleberry bushes toward the creek," I said. "There should be enough to make a couple of big batches of jam when they get ripe."

"And the peaches. Gruenfeld's orchard is only about ten miles south. As long as the orchard is still intact," Ted said.

"Will Max just let people take his fruit?"

"He and Betty have been living in the west camp since the start. Anne said he is happy to share his peaches. Otherwise, they would just rot. Besides, Kenton took him in. He's grateful for that."

I looked up at the sun and realized it was close to noon. "I better get going, Ted. Missus Marsh will be needing another bucket of beets soon."

"You better not disappoint her. I heard the beans should start coming in a few days from now," Ted said.

"Another item to add to the menu," I said. "And three deer being butchered, so meat will be more plentiful soon."

"Does Buck think he can keep a steady supply of venison?"

"I haven't talked to him," I said. "I don't really know him."

Ted nodded. "That's fine, I'll see if I can talk to Clint."

I headed back to the beet field as I considered what had happened. I had always assumed we would need the police and the police would enforce the laws that kept us safe.

But did we need them? It was clear our only law officer was not going to do what was expected. So did we need him?

And if we didn't, what was keeping us from devolving into animals…. burning and looting our town? The answer I came to was Lester. I realized Lester, of all people, would be the head of one of those groups that took what they wanted and didn't care if others were hurt. But his group wasn't doing it either. Lester and his group had hope. Hope that they could not only survive, but that they could continue living. And that is what Ted had given Kenton as well.

He had convinced us, in the first hours of our first day, of our new reality; that we could survive no matter how bad it got. He convinced us he had a plan to get us past the issues with water and food. When people started breaking, instead of going wild and thinking they had nothing to lose, they looked to the leadership Ted had established.

The council had always confused me to this point. I didn't understand why Ted needed a formal declaration of who his advisors were. He was our de facto leader, he could take counsel from whomever he chose.

But a council gave people a sense there was a structure of authority. That there was a system of responsibility. That there was a sense of normality. All of those illusions let people see even though today might be a struggle, there were plans for tomorrow and next week and next month and next year.

That sense of long term planning gave hope. And hope kept people working.

I realized work had kept me from doing foolish things myself. I had thought several times about trying to go and find Lexi and Emma on my own, but there was always something immediate to hold me here. If it wasn't digging onions and beets, it was digging latrines or spreading information to others.

If I had left in the first few days, I wouldn't have been in good enough shape to make it. Those first days, it was only the loan of Clyde from Anne that let me travel around town. My legs grew stronger and my pot belly shrunk in the first couple of weeks, but I still wouldn't have had the strength I did now.

And now… now I wondered if it was too late. If I left today, would it be a useless endeavor? I had to trust they had found a way to survive, they had found a group who would take them in, and they had found a way for hope to shine on their lives.

I picked up a bucket at the Marsh's house and went to the field to start digging more beets. A few girls were out in one row. They talked as they gathered, so I settled myself two rows over. The ground had firmed up a bit since I had left and it was actually easier to dig the roots out. I kept thinking about what had held me in Kenton for so long. It had been two weeks since I was given the radio to fix, but shouldn't I have left before then? Self-doubt and guilt ate away at my spirit as I went about the task at hand.

I kept telling myself it would turn out okay. Once I fixed the radio, I would be able to contact someone near Chicago and eventually talk to Lexi and Emma.

The bucket of beets was full before I was through with my thoughts and I carried it over to the group of women preparing dinner.

"David," Millie said. "I think you need to go home and rest."

"I'm fine, Missus Marsh."

"No, you need to go rest, David. You look like you aren't feeling well."

I was angry. Of course I didn't feel well. I was hungry, my muscles ached, and my wife and daughter were two-hundred and fifty miles away from me.

"Thank you, Missus Marsh. I might just do that."

"I'll send someone over with your dinner tonight. Just... just get some rest."

I smiled at her and turned to go. I almost ran into Sarah as I turned. Her eyes grew big and her mouth dropped open. She scrambled back. Her expression and movements were frightened, as if I was prepared to pounce on her. I nodded to her and walked away.

Maybe I felt bad after all. Maybe I looked sick. I wasn't sure. I would check when I got home. I thought I probably needed a bath. That would be a bucket of water to pull across the street. And I would want to put on some fresh clothes afterward. I would feel better after a bath and change of clothes.

Dad was in the garage when I arrived home.

"Hi Dad," I said as I picked up a bucket.

"Hello, Son," he said. "Is everything alright?"

"Yeah. Missus Marsh told me to come home and rest. I must look sick."

"That must be it," Dad said. "Your Mom is resting in our room. Looks like you're going to take a bath. Just don't wake her if possible."

I didn't know what kind of racket he thought I would make, but I held in my terse retort and just smiled and nodded.

I was relieved I didn't have to wait at the pump. Most people gathered their water in the morning and a little before the sun went down. The evening pump time was usually the time when people shared news and rumors. It had become a socializing event and often there were those who showed just for the gossip and information. Happily, none of them were there when I gathered the water for my bath.

Dad wasn't in the garage when I returned, nor did I see him as I carried the water into the bathroom. I went into my bedroom and gathered some clean clothes. As I turned to go back to my bath, I caught a glimpse of myself in the mirror above my dresser.

There was a stranger in the glass looking back at me. Gaunt and tired looking, covered in mud, the stranger wore my face. This man looked like me, but he was angry. Not frustrated or in a rage, just angry. Resentful.

This is why Missus Marsh and Dad asked me if I was alright. This is why Sarah shrank back from me and Dad told me to be careful not to disturb Mom. The man I was staring at was ready to break.

I took a deep breath, closed my eyes and forced my face away from the mirror. I could break later. Right now, I needed a bath and some clean clothes.

THIRTEEN

"David."

I sat up and looked around. I was in the middle of a dream and my dad's voice cut through. It wasn't loud, but it had a very insistent tone.

"David."

"I'm up," I said. Too loud. Not so loud. "What's wrong?"

My eyes adjusted to the faint light. It was a good while before dawn, but the sun was already lighting the world.

"Come on, get dressed. Hurry."

I looked at Dad and was surprised. He was fully dressed and he had a rifle in each hand.

I reached over and grabbed the jeans I had hung over the back of my desk chair.

"What's going on?" I asked. A yawn hit me as I continued. "Why do you have guns?"

"Trouble south," Dad said. "Three shots and then Farrin came tearing by on his motorcycle. Listen."

I stopped pulling up my jeans and listened carefully. I could hear the bell from the town ring over and over.

"What kind of emergency?" I asked.

"Don't know, but we need to go." Dad turned and walked out the door.

I grabbed my shoes and put them on. I didn't take the time to find a clean shirt, I just grabbed the t-shirt I had tossed on my laundry hamper the night before and hurried to catch up with Dad.

There were small groups of men, and more than a few boys, walking down Granger with rifles and shotguns.

Buck Fredrickson and his two older boys were a hundred feet ahead when I fell in beside Dad.

"They must have been sleeping with their guns to get here before us," Dad said as he handed me a rifle.

"There must be twenty men on the road. Do we need this many?"

"Maybe not, but always better to have more than you need than not enough."

I squinted in the grey light and tried to look farther down the road. The summer humidity had already taken hold and mists were common in the early hours of the morning. Ahead I thought I saw something darker though, a smudge of gray that hung too heavy.

"I think that's smoke," I said as I pointed down the road.

"I think you're right," Dad replied. "We're upwind or we could tell for sure."

Buck and his boys picked up their pace and soon they trotted ahead of us. Buck was a large guy, though not as much as when I first saw him on Dad's front lawn that first night. He moved quickly when he wanted to. I had heard from several people he could move swift and silent in the woods.

He had been in the military for a couple of tours. Part of some special unit from the rumors. Dad didn't know more than his military service and I had never spoken to Buck for more than a few minutes.

The sky kept growing brighter as we walked and soon we could see the bridge over Carter's Creek. The town's barricade was in the middle of the bridge and there was a gathering of men crouching behind the obstruction. More men were behind the structure of the bridge. They motioned people where to go when they approached.

A thick pillar of smoke rose from beyond the barricade. It looked like something was burning in the road not far on the other side of the bridge. As we drew near, we could hear an exchange of shouts and calls.

Buck and his boys had reached the bridge and huddled down behind the thick concrete that made up the culvert. Buck moved in a careful crouch up toward the barricade.

"Pat, over here."

I turned to see Luke motion us over to the side of the road.

"Come on," he said as we joined him. "There is a good spot near the river with plenty of cover."

"What's going on?" Dad asked as he followed Luke.

"A gang or something from the south. They said they had something to show the town. I don't know what it was, but there was some terrible screams and one of the boys at the barricade fired the alert shots."

"I heard the shots," Dad said. "Woke me up. But then there was another shot and about a minute later Farrin went tearing past the house heading into town. He got the bell ringing."

"Don't know what the other shot was," Luke said. "I just threw on my boots, grabbed my rifle and headed to the bridge."

There was a fallen tree that rested against a larger tree near the river. Luke guided us to the location and pointed at the far side of the bridge.

"There they are," he said. "Not even hiding behind cover."

A group of men stood on the south side of the bridge. I guessed the closest was just over four hundred feet from me and the furthest maybe another twenty or twenty-five. Several of them looked over to where we positioned ourselves and smiled. All of them had rifles in their hands and at least two handguns hanging on their belt. They looked dirty and smelly, their clothes a mixed collection of whatever would be cool enough in the heat and yet rugged enough for outside living.

A tall one was yelled something up at the barricade. He pointed back at a wooden structure that smoldered and put up a ton of smoke. It looked like it was a stack of four or five tractor tires with something stuck in the middle.

"Dear God," Dad said. "That's a man they set on fire."

"What?" Luke asked. "Is that what is burning?"

The tall man raised his rifle over his head and yelled something. He pointed back at the burning stack of tires and the other men with him cheered and laughed.

"I think it's a threat," Dad said. "They must want or need something from us."

"I wonder—"

Luke's question was cut short as the crack of a rifle shot pounded into my ears. I dropped to the ground as a barrage of gunfire thundered through the morning air. I looked up to see that both my Dad and Luke had taken shelter behind trees, their rifles ready to raise. My gun lay in the mud where I dropped it.

"Hold fire! Hold fire!" someone called from the bridge.

I looked over the fallen tree and saw the men who had been taunting and laughing at their murderous activities. They all lay unmoving in an area of the road that looked as if it had been painted the brightest red I had ever seen.

Dad and Luke were both swore under their breath as they hurried over to the bridge.

I stood shocked as I watched several men carefully walk down the bridge and examine those who lay still. Buck walked down and stared at the burning tires.

I picked up the rifle and walked slowly toward the gathered and animated group of men from Kenton. There were about forty at the bridge when I arrived and dozens more were coming down the road from town.

"Come on, David," Dad said. "Let's get home before your mother worries about what happened."

Dad was angry about something. Probably the senseless waste of life. I was embarrassed by my reaction along the bank of the creek and wanted to find something I could help with.

"You go on, Dad. I want to see what I can do to help."

He held his hand out and looked at the muddy rifle I held. I handed it to him and he took it without a word and started north along the road.

I walked through the jumbled crowd of men with guns until I came to the barricade. The men who were killed were being dragged off the road into a small grassy area. Buck seemed to be in charge of the clean up as he pointed at a body and then pointed where he wanted it placed.

Two men from Kenton were trying to move the burning pillar of tires. The stack of tires was on some sort of wheeled sled, but the heat from the burning rubber kept them from getting close enough to grab the handle.

"Do we know who that was?" I asked myself.

"Bill Ellison, from what I was told," Luke said. He had come up beside me as I watched the horrific scene on the other side of the bridge.

"What?" I asked.

"You asked who was burning. Right?"

"Yeah, but I didn't realize I had asked out loud."

"I talked with one of the men who were at the bridge when these fellows showed up. They were pulling something with them, but it was covered with a large piece of canvas, like a drop cloth. When they stopped, they pulled it off and Bill was standing in the tires. He was beat up real bad and they had tied his hands in front of him and to the top tire. They had duct taped his mouth shut, too."

"What happened?"

"The men asked if the town needed some entertainment. Then they wrapped the drop cloth all around Bill, poured a bottle of something on it, and lit him up. Charlie fired the warning shots in the air and those fellows just laughed and asked him if he wanted others to come and see. They seemed surprised when Farrin ran off the bridge and jumped on his motorcycle. They laughed as he pulled away. The men here wanted to go down and help, but those fellows lowered their rifles and told them to watch. The fire eventually burned enough of the tape off to let Bill scream. Charlie pulled up and fired a shot into his head. Likely spared him a few minutes of agony."

"Those men didn't fire back?"

"No, I think they were waiting till more people showed up. They could have killed everyone at the barricade when they first arrived, so I don't think that was why they came."

"If they weren't going to fire on us, why bring guns and murder Bill?" I asked.

"To tell us they meant business," Buck said.

I turned to see the grizzled hunter standing on the other side of the barricade.

"What business?"

"Were you close enough to hear?"

I shook my head and Luke grunted a "No."

"That one I shot in the face, I asked him where Stacy and the girls were. He told me they were down in Thayer being treated like little queens," Buck said. "That's when I shot the jackass."

"I don't get it," Luke said. "Why?"

"Because whoever is in charge down in Thayer, or wherever the girls are, was only interested in the question 'Will they defend themselves?' When his boys here don't come back, he will have his answer and leave us alone."

"You know that?"

Buck pulled out a cigarette and lit up as he looked at Luke.

"Yeah, I know that. Whoever is in charge down there sent some of his troublemakers up here to see what would happen. If they had made it back, they would be up here time and time again. Pushing us around, taking what they wanted. Any vehicles? Gone. Women and girls? Gone. Food? Gone. Medicine? Gone. If they knew we were too much of a bunch of daisy dancers to shoot them when they murdered one of our own in front of us, they would know they had us by the balls anytime they wanted anything."

"Sounds like you have thought about this, Buck," I commented.

"I have. When I was walking the woods looking for game, I thought a lot about what we might have faced on a day like today. When moron there mentioned the girls were back somewhere waiting for them, it let me know he answered to someone who had enough power to send him away. And since they brought Bill back from where he came from, it let me know whoever sent him wanted it to get personal."

"Still a lot of guessing in there," Luke said.

"See a car?" Buck asked.

"Well, no."

"How did they get here?"

"I guess they walked," Luke said.

"With no food or water? No packs? They dragged Bill and those tires all the way from Thayer? That's thirty miles. Bill and his family left six days ago. Figure an hour to get to Thayer, the rest of the day to be caught and raped. That leaves five days and four nights for them to get him back here with no food or water. That's a lot to ask while dragging that thing."

"Okay, then how did they get here?" I asked.

"Cars. They pulled up last night after sun down around the bend in the Highway. There the morons get out, rig up their little fire display, pop Bill inside, and pull it down the road right before dawn. They are told they will be picked up after they get done."

"Then we should go wait for them to come back and ambush them," I said. "Maybe we can get the cars and go and rescue the girls."

"They ain't coming back. Like I said, these fellows were troublemakers sent to die. If we had given in, they would have gone back to their pickup point and waited. After a day or two they would have walked back down the highway to their town. Maybe they would have been shot on sight, maybe they would have been kept around, but whoever is in charge would have known we could be pushed around."

"So what happens now?" asked Luke.

"In a few days, they will likely send someone to take a peek at our little barricade here. If it is well manned, they will leave us be, I would guess. There are other places where they can get what they want without getting all shot up. Who knows, they might come to us looking for legitimate trade eventually."

"Buck!"

All three of us turned to see who had called to him. It was Ike Stokes. He had been the postmaster from over in Wilcox, but lived in Kenton. Now he was one of the town council. He was stalking up the bridge in a fury.

"I understand you're responsible for this carnage," Ike said. "Well?"

"I shot first, that's true. I fired another eight times as well. Emptied my magazine."

"Did they fire back?"

Buck shook his head and ran his hand through his hair. "Nope. Didn't really want to give them a fair fight. Just wanted to kill them."

Ike glanced over at the red stained road. "I think the council needs to hear what happened. We won't stand for anyone taking matters like this into their own hands."

"Didn't have time to bring it up in a meeting, Ike. Something had to be done and I did it."

"Well, let's go. You can tell it to the council and we will figure out what should happen."

Buck pulled the pistol from his belt and held it out to Ike.

"What's this for?"

"I figure you wanted me unarmed, didn't you?"

Ike smiled a little. He took the firearm, turned and walked off the bridge.

"I guess you better get going," Luke said.

"I guess I should," replied Buck.

He hopped over the barricade and followed the councilman down the road. His boys came over to him and he gave them his rifle, another handgun and three knives before they trotted out into a field.

"What do you think is going to happen?" I asked Luke.

"Not sure. He seems pretty certain he saved us from a dangerous group, but I'm not sure if his story will hold up with the council. At the same time, he is the best of the hunters and having venison on the menu has made everyone happier."

"So they could just let the death of a bunch of strangers slide because he can keep our bellies full."

"I've seen worse injustice in my life," Luke muttered. "Well, let's go back to my place David. I have something that you might can use."

"What?"

"A pile of old electronics."

"I'll take a look, but don't get your hopes up."

Luke dropped a big arm across my shoulders. "David, what you are doing is just as important as what happened here today. If you can get that radio working, then you expand our world from beyond what we can see."

FOURTEEN

The box I carried was loaded with junk. Most of it had sat up in attics or in boxes at the back of closets. Luke had been in charge of going to each house in the three southern sections of town to make sure there was no one with problems they may not want to share with others. He had a good way of pulling information out of strangers after just a few minutes.

There was the family who had a child with a thyroid condition. They didn't know what to do because the follow up visit to determine a course of treatment was scheduled for the week after the EMP hit. Luke was able to get Bill Hanson to talk with them and look at the boy. He was able to find a medicine that would work that wasn't prioritized. Luke was also able to get several of the older single men and women to move into houses together. He said it was for them to keep an eye on each other, but I knew it was to keep loneliness from becoming a real problem.

While he went on those visits, he also asked people about what books they had. It was surprising the number and types of books some families had in their houses. Most were entertainment or biographical, but a few were books turned up some very useful information. A few handbooks from the Boy Scouts and other organizations like that had first aid, water gathering and other basic survival skills. Enough people had remembered what they had learned that the books weren't essential, but they were being passed around and studied by those who felt they could use the extra know-how.

Luke had also asked people if they had any older electronics lying about. Anything from before the 70's in particular. Most people didn't, but a few had some old televisions, clocks, calculators, and most importantly, radios that were gathering dust.

The box had to weigh at least sixty pounds, but I carried it with ease. One of the few silver linings from this situation was everyone seemed to be getting into good shape. Those that had survived.

Luke had showed me his collection of pieces and I had spent a good two hours on the floor of his living room as I sorted out what I thought might be useful to me. I was able to cut and strip out yards of wiring of different thickness, find all sorts of components that looked like they might still function, and see different configurations of systems that might give me an insight on how to fix the radio.

I didn't want to get my hopes up, but I was excited to get home and start taking all of my new-found treasures out of the box.

I entered through the front door and noticed Mom was not in her customary spot on the couch. Dad's head peeked around the corner of the hallway. He looked upset and I was sure it was the killings that morning that had put him in a foul mood.

He sighed and relaxed when he saw me.

"Davey," he said as he stepped into the living room. He held a pistol in his right hand.

"Dad, what's wrong?" I asked.

He motioned toward the kitchen with a jerk of his head and slipped the pistol into a holster that hung on his belt.

I shifted the box and turned slightly. The kitchen door leaned against the counter by the sink. The frame where the door normally hung was splintered where the hinge once was. I put the box on the ground and dashed over to the doorway. The door had been knocked clear off its hinges, but I saw it had been knocked down from the inside, not kicked in from the garage like I had expected to find.

"What happened?" I turned to find Dad had slipped up right behind me.

"Someone broke in and when your mother confronted them, they burst out the kitchen door and took off running."

"Is she okay?"

"Yes. But she's shaken up quite badly. She is resting in bed right now. She slipped off to sleep a few minutes ago."

I was stunned. I felt like I had lost my mind. With everything that had happened, the idea Mom would have been in danger in her own house was something I never would have suspected.

"Wait. Someone broke into the house while Mom was here?"

Dad nodded.

"What happened? I mean, Mom may have been able to chase me around with a switch when I was a kid, but…"

Dad's face softened as he smiled for a second.

"She had this in her hand," he said patting the pistol at his waist.

"You keep that in the nightstand by your bed," I said. "Where was she when he broke in?"

"She was still in bed. They broke in just a few minutes after we left for the bridge."

That was early. Very early in the morning.

"Was anything taken or broken?" I was worried they might have been here just to attack Mom.

"Yeah," Dad said. "They grabbed the medicine off the dresser."

"What medicine?"

"My heart pills and your mom's brain pills."

My breath caught in my throat.

"But you need that medicine," I said. I felt stupid for voicing the fact, but I was panicked.

"I know, Davey. And your mom needs hers. But we all knew we would run out eventually. I only had about a dozen pills in there, anyway. I was down to one every three days trying to stretch them out."

Ted's words about scavenging in other towns came back to me. I didn't want to think about it, but my folks both needed medication to live. I knew it had to be done.

"He ran out of the kitchen?" I asked.

"Uh, yes," said Dad. He was flustered by my sudden change of topics.

I hurried to the garage and looked for the container Dad had stored the aspirin he used to decoy Mom with. The container was missing.

"It's gone," I called back to the house.

"What is?" said Dad as he hurried through the kitchen.

"The aspirin out here," I said as he poked his head out of the kitchen doorway.

"I didn't even think to check out there," he said.

"Someone knew where we kept it."

"They've been spying on us?"

"Yes," I said. "They have been watching and waiting for the right time to break in. When we left this morning, they must have been near and seized the opportunity."

Dad frowned and put both of his hands on the top of his head. "Let's ask around and see if anyone else has had any medicine stolen."

I nodded. "I'll go do that. Did Mom get a good look at the man?"

"No. She couldn't describe him anyway. Maybe after her nap she can be of more help, but I think today is going to be a bad day. The shock of what happened sure isn't going to help in any case."

I examined the place where the hinges were tore out of the door frame. I didn't think it would be too easy to fix. I looked down in the garage and noticed the door and the man must have landed on the hood of Dad's car. The paint was scratched in several places and there was a noticeable dent on the front right fender.

"Think that will buff out?" Dad asked as he looked over my shoulder.

I laughed and thought back to when I was sixteen and had a small fender-bender with Dad's car in the school parking lot after a basketball game. When I got home, he went ballistic. He screamed and yelled at me. When we went inside, he told Mom I had 'wrecked the car'. She went outside to look at it and informed him she had popped the dent out and the scratches would buff out with a little elbow grease.

We both knew that wasn't true, but she had made us smile and soothed over the very contentious evening.

"Why did you run into Casey's car that night?" Dad asked. He was thinking of the same thing, apparently.

"Well…" I stumbled over the words. "Anne had just told me something, and it distracted me."

"She just told you something?"

"Yeah, she told me what she wasn't wearing under her skirt."

"Ah," Dad said. "Sorry I yelled at you, then. Come on, let's get a tarp up over this doorway. I'm going to shut and lock the garage door. We'll just have to use the front door from now on."

It was going to be a longer walk to the outhouse, but I agreed we needed to lock down access to our house. It saddened me that after weeks of feeling scared of starvation, disease and the loss of our normal lives, we now added criminal activity to the mix.

I shut the garage door and padlocked it while Dad found another tarp out in his toolshed. He brought in some woodscrews and a couple of screwdrivers and we set some anchor points for the tarp to attach to.

When we were done, I went to visit some of the neighbors to see what I could discover about our thief. None of the neighbors had seen anything that morning, the excitement at the bridge was what most wanted news about. But a few had noticed things disappearing. No medicine, but some tools, a few books, and even a small jewelry box with some inexpensive earrings and necklaces inside.

When I told them we had a break in and medicine was taken, they all seemed taken aback. Some of the men talked about forming a neighborhood watch, as if we didn't watch out for each other before, and most mentioned they would start locking their doors again. The age of community seemed to come to an end that afternoon in the south section of Kenton. All because we had someone with criminal intent on the loose.

It was noon by the time I made it to the Marsh's house and picked up a bucket for harvesting. Millie told me she needed help in the waxed and green bean field. I was happy to be picking a new crop. Every new food we added to our diet was an added defense against malnutrition and vitamin deficiency. At least that is what the books said. I think most people looked forward to the first wheat harvest. The lack of bread was the primary complaint from everyone.

I understood why those in the olden days would have huge celebrations at harvest time. It was survival. A good harvest meant food for the future. It meant there would be a future. I imagined the celebration we would throw at the first wheat harvest would seem like the Pilgrim's first Thanksgiving.

The rows of beans seemed full and bushy after the substantial rain we had. I had chosen to pick them facing away from the wheat and corn fields because I knew they would distract me as I worked. A few of the younger teens, who were working the field with me, asked how I gathered so many beans in such a short while. So, when I went back with a fresh bucket, I showed them how to gather. My grandmother had taught me when I was a child and I was amazed at how everything came back to me.

Yellow wax beans and long green beans filled my bucket and I thought about how many would be going into the daily stews and meals and how many we would have to can, jar and dry for the winter. I knew some of the retired farmers and hobby gardeners knew how many planting and harvesting seasons we would need of each plant, but how many people could be fed through the winter months? That was my concern.

Beyond that, we needed a steady supply of meat. We needed chickens for eggs, cows for milk, and pigs to slaughter. All of these animals surely had to be available somewhere but, as Ted had pointed out, because the big factory farms of these animals did not have a ready source of feed, most of the animals were likely dead from starvation anyway.

There were a few dairy cows on some outlying farms, but those cows couldn't produce enough milk for 5,000 people. Nor could the pigs that were available feed that many. We needed more food, and that meant either barter with a group that had those animals or taking them from those we didn't mind taking from.

I didn't like it when my mind turned to these dark thoughts. I had not believed myself capable of seriously considering raiding for things we needed.

"What's got you frowning and picking beans like they are fingers of people you hate?" asked Kenny.

"Someone broke into our house today."

Kenny looked up from where he was kneeling. "Broke in? Did they take anything?"

"Yeah. Dad's heart pills, what was left of them anyway, and Mom's pills for her condition."

"That's horrible. Anything else?"

"Some aspirin."

"Did anyone see them?"

"Mom did. She was in bed when he broke in and ended up in her bedroom."

"Oh my God. Is she alright?"

"Yeah. She pulled the gun from the night stand and chased him out of the house."

Kenny twisted his lips. "She should have shot him then and there."

"I don't know if my Mom could have done that."

"She better be glad he didn't know that, then. If he suspected she didn't have it in her to shoot, he may have tried to take the gun from her. Better to kill a thief in the act then to let him go on stealing. What most people don't get about stealing is it is killing. I didn't understand that when I was a young buck. Heck, I wasn't even young when I turned from my old life. I was 38 before I realized what I was doing. By stealing, I was taking someone's life."

"Because they might have needed what you stole? Like my folks' medicine?"

"Nah, not even that straight forward. If I boosted a ring, let's say, I would justify it by saying their insurance would pay for it. But they paid the insurance company for their policy, so I was stealing from all the folks paying for insurance."

"But that's just money," I said. I was a little confused at what he was trying to explain.

"No, it's not just money, David. It's what they did to earn that money. They spent time doing whatever they did to earn that money. It's not even how hard they worked, I realized. It was the time. If I stole something they spent five hours earning, I stole five hours of their life. I stole their life, man. Time is the only thing we can't replace, and a thief takes that from you."

"I never thought about it that way."

"Most people don't. But more need to, now. We aren't living in a world where insurance or police or courts can give you back even your money. But time is even more precious now. Time is all we have to give or to lose. And someone who steals your time steals a double portion of your life. He takes the time you have already spent, and takes some time you will spend just getting back to where you were. Thieves and murderers are one and the same in this new world."

A cold shiver ran down my back as Kenny's words sank in. We were no longer in a place where an outside force could protect us. It was every man for himself in a very real sense. Kenton had held together, but it was more out of instinct than thought. Although most people in town were the type to look out for their neighbors, there were always some that sought to take advantage when they could.

A few men had been roused from their afternoon naps over the last few weeks and given jobs to do. But, as the frantic pace had slowed down, more and more were finding less and less motivation to work.

Buck and his hunters would always be out in the woods hunting, but they would be even if the event hadn't happened. That's just who they were. Others would be tending their gardens and eating out of their back yards, true, but how many people would be hauling water for laundry or picking beans if they didn't have to?

I looked down at the bucket at my feet. It was filled halfway with long green beans. Enough to feed me and my folks for a few days at least. But I didn't gather these just for my family, I gathered them for the women who cooked and washed clothes. I gathered them for the men who stood guard over our roads. I gathered them for the men and women who dug graves. But I also gathered them for the men who slept late and found excuses not to work. It wasn't right, but as long as I did what I felt was right, they would eat. What would happen if I stopped picking for them? I feared they would seek to take what they weren't given. And in that aspect, Kenny was right. We lived in a town with murderers all around us.

FIFTEEN

The next morning I left the house and headed into town on foot. Ted had asked Anne and me to go out to his house and help him with a special project. I had arranged for Sarah to take my place in the bean field the evening before, so I had been able to sleep in a little before I left home to meet up with Anne at the library.

I was interested in seeing where Ted and Kenny lived. I knew Kenny's sister and her kids were up there, but Ted indicated there were a few other people that had been gathered in as well. Dad had promised he would let Luke do any strenuous work if he needed it, but I still felt uncomfortable leaving the house for an entire day.

I closed my eyes as I walked and breathed deep. I soaked in the late morning air. It was that time of late-June when the mornings were cool but the afternoons became hot and humid. The edge of coolness was gone and I enjoyed the comfortable warmth. In my high school days, this would have been a day to go to the pool or to the pond at Anne's house. You could tell the late afternoon would be a scorcher, but most of the day would be lazy and relaxing.

I waved at the people in the field. Some smiled and waved back, but others scowled and went back to their work. Those were the ones who always complained when someone arranged for a day of other work. They also tended to be those whose buckets were never quite full.

I looked at the patchwork of crops and sighed. Full, bountiful rows of carefully tended crops were producing more food each day. The right amounts of rain and sunshine combined with the hard work put forth by the people of the south section of Kenton were producing more food than we needed to survive at the moment. The canning of beets and beans would start in a few days and that would be the first steps we needed to take to survive the winter.

I noticed there was a steady stream of people moving toward the town center. As I got closer, I saw there was a knot of people in front of Sorenson's Auto Body Shop. At the center was Kenny. Deputy McDaniels was behind him and pointed to several places while he yelled.

"What's going on?" I asked a woman as she walked passed me. She was visibly upset as she walked away from the group.

"They are going to hang him unless the council gets here soon," she said. "I'm surprised McDaniels hasn't just shot him yet."

"Who?" I asked. I looked back at Kenny who was in the middle of the crowd.

"That black guy. The one Riggins is friends with. He killed someone they say."

I ran toward the crowd. I didn't know what I could do when I got there, but I was not going to waste time walking.

As I closed in on the group, I could see a blanket laying over something in the street. I knew immediately it was a body and felt my chest constrict in panic and rage.

"David!" Kenny called as I came close.

"What's going on here?" I asked.

"Your friend murdered Talley," McDaniels said. "We don't have a jail, and we can't have a killer running free, so I'm thinking we just hang him from the same lamppost he hanged Brent on."

"Kenny, you didn't hang him, did you?"

"Sure did. Hanged him, put the sign around his neck, and sat here for people to see."

I was stunned. It felt like the world spun as I tried to keep my feet.

"Why?"

"He was a thief. I caught him breaking into the Foster's house. I chased him back to this here auto body shop and beat him unconscious. Then I searched his locker in the back and found all sorts of stuff that weren't his. Like your folk's medicine."

"Is that true?" someone in the crowd asked.

"Was Brent Talley a thief?" another voice called out.

"If he hanged a thief, then good!" a woman yelled.

McDaniels waved the crowd quiet. "I told ya'll what I would do if it were my choice, but our good mayor has decided the council that his friend has set up will decide. Does that seem like justice to you?"

Some of the crowd yelled in support of killing Kenny right then, while others shouted the council should decide.

A crack in the air like thunder had me drop to one knee by instinct. Others had fallen prone and several in the crowd were crouched. Most, however, stood where they were and looked around. Ted stepped through the crowd with his rifle held high in the air. I hoped he wasn't foolish enough to have fired his gun into the air as that bullet had to come down somewhere.

"Thank you Deputy McDaniels. I understand you have taken the statement and have examined some evidence," Ted said as he walked toward Kenny and the law man.

Anne was part of the group that followed in Ted's wake through the crowd. The council stood in a rough semi-circle around Ted, Kenny and the deputy. Anne came and stood by me.

"Is it true?" she asked quietly.

I nodded. "I think so."

"Alright, let's take the prisoner over to the mayor's office," Ted said. "I think we will need a trial to decide what should happen."

Ted saw me as he turned to leave.

"David, you and Anne need to go up to my place. Tell Tom you are the ones that are going to help us."

"Okay, Ted," I said. "Is this going to change anything?"

"This changes everything," Ted said. He sighed and for the first time he looked tired and weary to me. "I wish he had come to us with his suspicions or evidence. I knew he was going to go looking for the thief, but I had no idea what his plans were if he caught him."

"What will happen?" asked Anne.

"I guess we'll find out," said Ted.

I felt empty as I watched the crowd melt away as Kenny, Ted, and the others headed across the square to the city offices. My eyes were drawn to the body under the sheet laying in the street. I had seen too many dead bodies in the last few months. Before the event, I had only seen a dead body in a coffin at a funeral. The queasy and uncomfortable feelings I had experienced even in those circumstances were a distant memory. And yet looking at the lumpy outline of Talley's body, I felt sick and my heart ached. Not for the thief who threatened my parents life. Not for the thief that callously put himself before all others. But for Kenny who did what he thought was right and now must see if others agreed with his decision.

"Come on, David," said Anne. She put a hand on my shoulder and turned me to her. "We need to go. We can't do anything here."

Anne was always pragmatic. While I often slipped into the miasma of 'what if', Anne had always looked at the choices before her without sentimentality. It was a life I couldn't imagine, and to this point was one I didn't think was better. Right now, it was better.

I turned and followed her as she led the way toward the library where Bonnie stood saddled and ready.

"They are still using Clyde to help augment the tractors," she said. "Honestly, I think he loves it. I think he likes working hard alongside so many people."

"It's strange, isn't it? Who would have thought an animal would find work like that enjoyable?" I asked as I walked with her. My eyes drifted to the small building that housed the city offices.

"David, stop looking," Anne chided me. "You will just get worked up. Ted asked us to go to their house and help Sophia with something. I don't think we need to mention what happened here today, and if you sink into melancholy, they will ask you what's wrong. So slap on a smile and let's get this done."

She mounted Bonnie in a single motion. I was surprised when she offered her hand to me.

"I'll just walk along side," I said.

"No you won't. I want to get there within the hour, and it will take twice as long if you walk."

I took her hand and pulled myself up behind her.

"There, now just don't grope me and you won't have any reason to feel guilty."

I stammered as I tried to defend myself. "I don't feel guilty. I mean, there is nothing for me to feel guilty about."

Anne shook her head and sighed. Then with a click of her tongue and a touch of her feet to Bonnie's flanks, we were trotting down the road out of town.

"David, I wish I could convince you it's alright if we're friends," she said as we made the turn onto the highway.

"I know that."

"Do you? Because for the last twenty-two years you have pretended I wasn't part of your life."

"I'm not the one who said I didn't want to speak with you again."

"I'm sorry. I shouldn't have said that. I was an angry seventeen year old girl and you were the boy who wouldn't fight for me."

I didn't know what to say. Those days were behind me, buried beneath years of life. I didn't want to dig them up again and fight with ghosts from my past.

"I just don't want to deal with it, Anne."

"I bet," she said.

I could hear the venom in her voice. She was upset and it was going to be a long ride out to Ted's place.

"Is this why you and Lexi are on the outs? You just don't want to deal with it?"

I jerked back as if she had burned me. Bonnie felt my shift and slowed her gait.

"What do you mean by that?" I asked.

"Your dad told me you were going through a rough time with her. Let me guess, she is all mad at you and you just ignore her to stop from fighting."

"Dad told you? I didn't tell him."

"People can see, David. They have eyes and they know you. They know when you are hurting and they can figure out what the issue is by the way you don't talk about it." She yelled the last five words from over her shoulder at me.

"What am I supposed to do? Have fight after fight with her? I don't even know what she wants."

"Yes, fight with her. Have her express what she is unhappy about. Express to her what you are unhappy about."

"I don't want to yell at her, I love her."

"Then be strong enough to let her yell at you. She doesn't want to be quiet, does she?"

I realized I had started to sulk. I didn't like when I did this, but I never knew what else to do.

"No, she is quite verbal with her displeasure," I said finally.

"And when she is displeased, do you let her just be displeased or do you try to fix it?"

"I try to fix it."

"She wants you to tell her she is just going to be displeased, David. She knows you can't fix everything and it frustrates her when you try. Just tell her it isn't anything you can fix but you will get through it together."

That didn't make any sense to me. And how did Anne know what Lexi wanted anyway? They never met each other. Well, maybe once or twice just after we were married.

"Have you talked to Lexi?" I asked.

"Don't be stupid, David. I've never spoken to Lexi except once many years ago."

"Then how do you know what she wants?"

"It's what I wanted, David. I know how you deal with conflict. And it isn't the way I want you to. I assume you picked a girl somewhat like me, at least that's what your dad says. And if that is true, then I understand what drives her crazy about you."

"Is that why you got mad at me? Because I wouldn't yell at you?"

She was quiet for a few minutes.

"Yes. That was part of it. My father had no right to threaten you. You weren't bad for me and he knew that. He just didn't want to think of his little girl growing up."

"I realize now it was just a threat, although at the time I was convinced he would kill me. But since I was heading off to college, don't you think you would have lost interest in me anyway?"

"I don't think so. I never did lose interest. I waited for you to call me every day. For years."

"You could have called me, you know?" This was not a conversation I wanted to have, but I knew she wouldn't let it drop.

"I couldn't call you, you would have thought I was interested."

"You were interested."

"True, but it was your job as the man to call."

"Sounds a bit sexist."

"I'm old fashioned."

"And alone."

She tensed up and I knew I had scored a hit. I wasn't proud of it, but I wanted to end this conversation and I thought if I made it unpleasant for her, she would drop it.

"Yes," she said. "I'm alone. And that's because I didn't fight for what I wanted."

Anne turned Bonnie onto a small blacktop road from the main highway.

"How far are we from the place?" I asked.

Anne was seething with a barely contained fury.

"About two miles," she said. Her voice was strained and I thought I may have gone a bit too far.

The shaded black road led deeper into the old forest. The cool, moist trail up the hill was the perfect place to spend a sweltering summer day, but it was warm and cozy compared to the frigid aura that seemed to radiate from Anne. If the chill was anymore real, I would have had frostbite on my hands.

The blacktop ended and a gravel road led us the rest of the way to Ted's compound. Several children ran out to see us. I assumed they were Sophia's because they were black and I didn't think there was another black family living out in the wilderness north of Kenton.

"Get down," Anne said as she pulled Bonnie to a stop. "You can walk back."

"Anne, I'm sorry."

I slid off the saddle and reached up to help Anne down.

I didn't see her foot as she swung off the saddle and it caught me square on the side of the head.

I tumbled to the ground. Her heavy boots were right in front of me when I opened my eyes.

"Are you dead?" she asked.

"No," I said. Her boots seemed to split into two pair as I tried to pull myself up.

"Maybe next time." She turned and led Bonnie away from me.

I closed my eyes and laid back down. My shoulder seemed to ache, probably from when I hit the ground, but nothing like the headache I was experiencing.

"You must have pissed her off something fierce," a voice said above me.

I opened my eyes and squinted through the pain. A wrinkled face set behind a heavy beard and mane of pure white hair was smiling at me.

"Ready to get up?" the old man asked. He held his hand out to me. I grabbed it and felt him pull me up.

"You must be David," he said as he steadied me.

"I am, and you are?" I asked.

"Tom Pearson," he said. "Glad to meet you."

"Thanks," I said. "This where Ted lives?"

"This is his Shangri-La. Come on, I'll introduce you to everyone."

I followed Tom up the rough drive way past a tall wooden fence. It wasn't one of those professional looking fences, this looked like it had been pieced together over a period of several years. Some of the tall slats of wood looked fairly new, stained and weather-treated, but others looked decades old.

"Besides Ted and Kenny, there are Sophia and her kids, Ben and Karen, and Holly and me. Not many people, but we do what we can."

I was half-listening to Tom and half trying to work out the soreness in my neck when my guide into the compound stopped and swept his arms around as if to show me something grand.

And it was grand. I was looking down into a small valley that was sheltered on each side by high oak and cottonwood trees. Terraced gardens ran down the valley toward a large pond. The pond was fed by two small streams that pooled every fifty feet or so. Small bridges and walkways led to various small buildings and structures.

The sounds of animals brought life to the amazing painting of farm life in front of me. Geese and ducks swam in the pond, chickens picked at the hard ground in front of the buildings where several goats were keeping the grass shorn short. Two big golden retrievers were following Anne and the kids from the barn where the lowing of cows lent a richness to the entire spectacle.

"This is amazing," I muttered.

"It is," Anne said as she stepped up beside me. "Sorry about the boot to the head. It really was an accident. I didn't see you turn back to help me."

"Why did you leave me lying there?"

"Because Tom was already coming out and I was pissed at you."

"Fair enough," I said. I turned slowly and looked around at everything that was hidden in this little plot of wilderness.

"What is that?" I said as I pointed up.

"That's a cell tower," Tom said. "It's the reason Ted wanted you to come up here today."

SIXTEEN

The cell tower stood a good two hundred and fifty feet high. It topped out the trees by a good hundred feet, and yet with the heavy spring foliage, I didn't even notice it as we had come out to Ted's place.

"How far away is it?" I asked.

"About a quarter of a mile from the gate over there," Tom said as he pointed between two buildings. "Me and Ben cleared the path to it and have run the wires needed."

"What wires?" I asked as I turned back to the old man.

"To hook the radio up to. Once you get it fixed, we will be able to hook it up and let the cell tower broadcast it for us."

"Wait, I'm not even sure I can fix the radio," I said. "I just don't know… I don't know."

"Don't worry about it, David. Ted just wanted you to see what we got ready for you. Come here."

Tom led me to a small shed next to what looked like an old fashioned windmill. It turned without creaking, but looked like it should have been in a sepia tinged photo from the dustbowl era. He turned back to where I stood unmoved and motioned to me in a way that made me feel like a skittish dog being called after his new owner.

I went to the small shed and he opened the door for me. Inside was a small, sturdy table with a power cord that looked like it would plug into the radio I was working on. I had noticed there was no power cord in the package Ted had given me, but I thought it was just an oversight on his part. Apparently it was not.

"You have a steady source of power?" I asked.

I pointed to the cord when Tom raised an eyebrow at my question.

"Of course," he answered. "Hasn't Ted told you anything about this place?"

"He said him and Kenny and Kenny's sister lived up here and survived on what they grew and could make."

"I suppose that's true. But what we can grow and make is, well, it's pretty nice. We have wind power to supply us with electricity and pump our water. Our solar panels blew out in the EMP, but we were able to get the generators going again. As long as our propane and gasoline supplies hold out, we should be good."

"How much do you have?"

Tom tugged at his ear and squinted up into the sun. "Well… we haven't really told anyone that yet. Ted was pretty particular about that information not being available."

I understood. It would make them a target if word ever got out. If they had enough supplies to last eighteen months, some would think, then surely they can take me and my family in. But then those supplies drop to twelve months. And then another family, and it's down to nine months. Pretty soon, they have nothing left and everyone who showed up is mad because they thought they would be okay.

"I assume enough for an extended period of time," I said.

"That's a good estimate," Tom replied. "Come on, I'll show you the other part of why you are up here today."

I followed him out of the small shed and we headed down the hill a bit. A small black woman and Anne talked in the doorway of a house. They looked up and smiled as we approached.

"You must be Sophia," I said as I extended my hand.

She took it in a soft handshake and nodded. "I am. You're David?"

"Yes, it's a pleasure to meet you."

"Sophia was just about to show me what we will be taking back to the town," Anne said.

"Really? We are taking something back?" I asked.

"Come back this way," Sophia said.

She entered the house and led us back to a nice sized kitchen. Six large plastic tubs were stacked up on the counters.

"That is enough herbs for a few months we figure," Sophia said as she patted one of the big bins.

"Wow," said Anne. "Those are full of herbs?"

"Yep. Basil, oregano, rosemary, coriander, thyme, dill, and bay leaves. There is some fresh mint and new garlic bulbs in there as well. Should be able to start growing quickly."

"Why are you giving us all of this?" I asked.

"Being neighborly," Sophia said. "My kids were curious about what you folks were eating in town. We told them you were eating bland stews and raw vegetables. That made my kids feel bad because they are eating better than the kids in town. So we talked about what we could give that the whole town could use. We usually have more herbs than we can use, so that seemed to be something we could do to make your lives a little better."

"Thank you, Sophia," Anne said. "And thank your kids. This is a wonderful gift and I'm sure the whole town will appreciate it."

"You're welcome, and I hope we will see you again soon."

Tom helped me take the bins of herbs out to the front road. Anne went to get Bonnie and I was trying to figure out how we would be able to strap the bins to the saddle when Ted appeared. He had his rifle in his hand and Kenny's backpack slung over his shoulder.

"Hey Ted," Tom called. "Wasn't expecting you back this early."

Ted stopped and looked at Tom and then at me.

"I take it David and Anne had the good sense not to say anything," Ted said as he resumed his walk up the road.

"About what?" Tom asked.

"Kenny. He got himself in trouble."

Tom muttered a few choice words and then looked up at me. "We thought he might do something stupid," he said. "What happened? Did he catch the thief?"

I nodded. "Yeah, he caught him. Found a bunch of things that were stolen. So I guess you could say he caught him red-handed."

"So Deputy Dawg didn't like someone doing his job, huh? Doesn't surprise me."

"It wasn't so much the catching that got him in trouble," Ted said as he came closer. "It was the hanging that seems to have ruffled some feathers."

Tom's face drained of color until his white hair seemed vibrant in comparison.

"Hanging?"

"Yeah," Ted said. "Seems Kenny decided that it would be a good thing to hang the thief instead of just catching him. So he did. Then he sat under the body and waited until a mob formed and he almost got himself shot or hanged."

"Where is he now?" I asked.

"They have him locked in the pharmacy. Hanson has a room where all of the remaining medicines are locked up. They decided that would be the best place to put Kenny until the trial."

"At least they are going to give him a trial," Tom said. "I don't know if I would if I were in their place."

"He mentioned trying to find a thief?" I asked.

"Last night," Tom said. "He came in and packed a bag. Said he was going to go back to town and see if he could find who was stealing stuff. Guess he had a few people tell him about some thefts."

I felt guilty. I didn't know Kenny would act to stop the thefts in this manner.

"What's wrong, David," Ted asked. "You knew about this, or at least some of it. But you look like you were sucker punched."

"Sucker kicked is more like it," Tom said. "That little filly kicked him in the head while dismounting. She said it was an accident, but she was smirking as she walked away with him flopping in the dirt."

Ted laughed. "Are you okay?" he asked me. He looked at my eyes and I could see he was concerned as well as amused.

"Yeah, I'm okay," I said.

"Good, I need to go let Sophia know what is happening with Kenny. Wait for me and I will head back with you and Anne."

Ted headed into the compound with Kenny's bag and a heavy chore of letting Sophia know about her brother.

"It wasn't the kick to the head that made you look all sick," Tom said as Ted got far enough away not to hear. "It was something about Kenny. Am I right?"

"It was me and my big mouth," I said. "Kenny was working in the bean field yesterday. I don't know why he works in the south fields. It's so far for him to walk. Anyway, we were talking and I mentioned my folk's medicine had been stolen and my mom had been scared and shaken by whoever broke in. Kenny started soapboxing like he does. He said thieves were no better than murderers and we needed to punish them for what they did."

"That sounds like Kenny. You know, I have never smoked a cigarette. Have you?"

"What?"

"I said I've never been a smoker. Did you ever smoke?"

"I'm sorry Tom, I don't understand."

"The question is pretty straight forward, I thought."

"No, I've never smoked."

"You ever get onto people for smoking?"

"I don't think so. I've asked a few people not to smoke in my house before."

"That's about as far as I've gone. But you should hear my wife. She will nag a person to death over their habit."

"She used to be a smoker?"

"That's right. See, converts make the best zealots. Former smokers or alcoholics understand what they experienced and they want to help others break free of those addictions. Even when those who are partaking in the activities don't see it as a problem. Kenny is the same way about his former life."

"You mean he was a criminal?"

Tom nodded. "He would have denied it even until a few years ago, but he has come to realize that even though he was never caught or punished, he was still a liar and a thief."

"And so he thought Brent Talley couldn't be reformed?"

"I guess. I'm not sure. Maybe he saw something more dangerous in him than simple theft."

"Taking my parents medicine was more than simple theft," I said. "It was a sure way to make certain they would die."

Tom scratched at his beard. "Yeah, this has changed a lot of things. When you need something to survive, the rules of morality and ethics tend to bend and break."

"Some superficial things change, but basic principles still hold. Kenny didn't have the right to hang Talley."

'Who did? We accepted the death penalty as part of our justice system, even if you disagreed with it. If we had to put someone to death, who has the right to make that decision and then carry it out?"

"What are you two talking about?" Anne said as she led Bonnie out onto the road.

"Kenny," I said.

Anne bit her lower lip and readjusted a strap on the saddle that looked perfectly snug to me.

"Yeah, Ted came in and asked for a minute with Sophia. I took that as my signal to get Bonnie and get back to town."

"Ted is going back with us, he asked us to wait for him."

Anne smiled. "I'm sure you appreciate the extra company. We wouldn't want you to feel unsafe."

Tom cleared his throat and edged his way over to the entrance of their compound.

"I'll take that as my signal to, uhm, be somewhere else. You have a safe trip back to town. It was nice to meet you David, look forward to you bringing us a working radio."

I waved goodbye to the old man and sat down on one of the plastic bins.

"I am sorry about kicking you, David. Are you okay?"

"Yeah, I'm fine."

"Better get used to that question. I bruised up your face pretty bad. It's swollen and you might have a black eye tomorrow morning."

"Well you rang my bell pretty good," I said. My face did feel a little puffy and numb.

Anne handed me a canteen. "I didn't see you bring any water with you. That's a bad habit, you know. You need to find some canteens if you expect to make it to Chicago in one piece."

"How did you know I was thinking about Chicago?"

"You need Lexi and Emma back. You need to take care of them. Your parents shouldn't be who you need to care for, they have each other."

She was right. Sometimes I felt like I was speaking out loud when I had private thoughts. What if other people can read my mind? Is that how she knows what I am thinking.

"I do need to get to them. It's been almost three months, though. Did I miss the chance to help them? That question haunts me every day."

"You couldn't have reached them without waiting, David. If you had gone haring off after them, you wouldn't have made it far. Now you are stronger, more resilient. Now you would have a chance of making it to Chicago."

"Maybe you're right. I don't know," I said. I looked up at the sky, more to avoid looking at Anne and digging deeper into this conversation than anything else. It wasn't anyone's business when I was going back to find my family. And yet, it stabbed at me every day I stayed in Kenton.

"What's up there?" Ted asked as he joined us by Bonnie. "Vultures back?"

"Vultures?" I asked. "We have vultures around here?"

"On occasion."

"Let's get this gift back to town. We will probably be able to get them to the cooks in time to season tonight's food," Anne said. "That will give the town something better to think about than Kenny."

"Why did you leave?" I asked Ted as we lashed the bins to Bonnie's saddle.

"I am too good a friend of Kenny. Not enough objectivity. The council wants to pick a group of men to act as a jury and they didn't want me there to influence them."

"Did you get a read of what they were thinking?" asked Anne.

Ted shook his head. "No. One of the reasons I picked the men I did was they were calm and collected in the face of panic. They also had wide social circles and were connected to many different aspects of the town. The one thing none of them had, however, was any personal relationship with either Talley or Kenny."

"They were right to ask you to leave," I said.

"I agree," Ted responded. "I don't like leaving him there like that, but I need to stay out of it. Otherwise it will break down the trust the town has for the council."

We started back to town, a small caravan of three bringing gifts from a not so distant land. Trade goods packed in plastic. A gift from children who wanted to bring some happiness in a land of long sorrow.

Those same children were probably being told by their mother that one of the men who protected and took care of them was in some trouble and wouldn't be home for a while. I hoped it would just be for a while. I hoped Kenny hadn't left his home for the last time.

We walked along in silence, each of us mulling over the issues of the day.

"Ted, when do you think David should go to Chicago?" Anne asked.

"I'm not sure, I would expect he is ready to go now."

"I'm not planning anything like that," I said. I could hear the defensiveness in my own voice. "This is something Anne brought up. I haven't been thinking about it."

Ted's eyes narrowed as he looked at me. "For someone who doesn't say much and observes others, you are a bad liar."

"I'm not lying," I protested.

"Maybe not to me, but then to yourself for sure. You need to go, and soon, David. It's gnawing away at you."

"I've got to get the radio fixed first."

"Every time someone brings up the radio, David, you insist you don't know if you can fix it," Anne said. Her voice was like a blade on fire, it cut and burned all at once. "So now you can't go find your family until after you finish a job you didn't want and don't know if you can accomplish? It's an excuse, David, and you know it."

"I still have to think about my parents."

Ted shook his head. "No, you don't. Think if you had decided to postpone your trip by a week. Your parents would be down here and you up in Chicago. Would you have made the trip down here to find and take care of your parents? No. You would have prayed for them and hoped they would find friends and neighbors to help take care of them. You are not moving because of fear, David. And it's eating at you."

I felt more than a little attacked at this point. It seemed like they were ganging up on me.

"Did you plan to bring this up with me on this trip?" I asked Anne.

"Not really, we had talked about this, though, and felt you needed to hear it."

"Who has been talking about this?" I asked. I was furious and I could hear it in my voice.

"No one," Anne answered. She seemed to realize maybe she had gone too far. "Just me and Ted, and Kenny. And your dad. And Luke. And Missus Marsh."

"What?"

Ted laughed. "You were right, Anne. Get him a little off guard and he really opens up."

"What is that supposed to mean?"

"It means I can hear your real voice. You have a fire in you, David. I've seen it a few times, but you keep yourself too controlled. You are afraid of yourself."

I snapped my mouth closed. My jaw was so tight it hurt, but I wasn't going to rise to their bait.

Ted sighed and looked over at Anne. "If you haven't given it much thought, then I'll believe it. Just start thinking about it, okay?"

"And talk to your dad. He's worried about you and I know he wants Lexi and Emma safe."

I swallowed and told myself they just cared about me and wanted what was best. I didn't like them getting involved in my life, but at least I knew I could trust them.

"I will. I promise."

"Good," said Ted. "Let's get these spices delivered, then we can meet up at the library and see what is going on with Kenny."

SEVENTEEN

The expressions of gratitude for the herbs and spices ranged from a mild look of surprise to a giddy joy at being able to provide new flavors for the daily meals. A few people asked what it was like up at Ted's place. I didn't provide many details, but told them I understood how Ted and his people were prepared to live through an event like this.

When I only had two empty bins to carry, I went home to check on my parents before I headed back into town. When I entered the front door, I saw mom and Rose on the couch. Mom was working her cross stitch while Rose was busy with her knitting needles.

"Hi Mom, Missus Johnson," I said. "Sophia and her kids sent a bunch of herbs and spices down from their place. So, the meals should taste much better."

"That's wonderful," Mom said. "Oh, that was so kind of her."

"Why are you over here Missus Johnson? Just need a change of scenery?" I asked.

She wore a smile I knew held a lot of sadness and more than a little pity.

"Your father asked me to come over and keep your mother company while he is gone this evening?"

"That's right," Dad said as he walked into the living room. "I've been called and I must go."

He was dressed in a full suit and stood a little taller and straighter than I had seen in many years.

"Have a job interview?" I asked. "Look like you'll impress them."

Wilson Harp

EMP

"No." he blushed and waved his hand. "Ike came down and told me they wanted me for the jury tonight. I figured I had a nice suit, I should wear it. When else am I going to wear it?"

"That's true. Wait, they are having the trial tonight?"

Dad nodded. "Yeah, they are sending the Ford down here to take me to the library in a little bit. I told Ike I didn't think I could walk all the way into town and he said they would provide the limo." Dad laughed and shook his head. "A busted up 1944 Ford pickup is as close as we have to a limo service in town. What a world we have slipped back into."

"You sound cheerful for what is bound to be a tough night."

"I know," he looked over at Mom and Rose sitting on the couch. "I guess I should be more somber, but I'm sick of it. I broke into the bottle of brandy that's been up in the cabinet for years."

"You got that on your trip to France on your 25th anniversary," I said. I lowered my voice and stepped closer to him. "Are you drunk?"

"No," he said. "Just buzzed a little. I only had a couple of swigs."

I was stunned. I had never seen Dad drink before. I knew he had drank during his Navy years, but Mom hadn't wanted alcohol in the house and it never seemed like it was a big deal to not have it around. I remember I was a senior in high school when they took their 25th anniversary trip to Paris and came back with a small bottle of brandy. Mom said they bought it as a keepsake and Dad always said they would drink it on their 50th anniversary.

That had already passed and I suspected Mom's keepsake argument won the day.

The sound of the truck pulling up to the house pulled my attention away from my dad and the brandy.

"Pat, you're ride's here," Mom said. "Don't be gone too long."

"I won't be, Honey. Davey, you want a ride? I'm sure they won't mind."

I looked at Mom and she smiled and waved me on. I followed Dad out to the road where the rusted out truck waited for us. It was shaking so hard you could hear the windows rattling in their loose fittings. Dense smoke poured out of the decrepit tailpipe and it almost sounded like the vehicle had a chronic raspy cough.

"If you want a ride, David, you need to get in the back," said Clint as I walked over to the truck.

I nodded and smiled. I had grown up riding in the back of pickups. Way too dangerous for the modern world, but I guess we weren't in the modern world anymore. I pulled myself up on the bumper using the tailgate as leverage. That was not a prudent decision, because it felt as if the tailgate might give way with just an ounce more of pressure.

I was about to jump in when I saw the bed of the Ford already had a sizeable amount of passengers. Several boys, none more than seven or eight, and about half a dozen dogs were milling about in the rough metal pit. I climbed in and took a seat against the back of the cab.

The truck lurched forward and I thought it was going to stall the way it sputtered, but the engine righted itself and we went flying down the road. I realized we were probably not going more than thirty miles per hour, but this was the first time I had been in a moving vehicle in three months and I could not help but laugh. A dirty grey hound lay down across one of my legs and looked at me with his tongue hanging out. I smiled back at the dog. The sheer exhilaration of riding where the wind blew by and the fields drifted along was something I never even realized I missed.

The truck slowed as we headed into town. A three minute ride, like an amusement park roller coaster, and it was over. Twenty minutes saved and my legs were glad for it.

The truck jostled to a stop and kids and dogs started pouring out of the bed. The tailgate never came down, it was just like a mass escape over the rusty steel sides. I found my footing and stood up.

"Dangerous to ride in an open bed like that," Anne said. She looked up at me from the side of the truck. "Why don't you get out of there and join me? They are almost ready to start the trial."

I wanted to hop off the side of the truck like a young foolhardy teenager would, but I decided a broken ankle wouldn't impress Anne much and would cause considerable problems for my own well-being. Why did I want to impress Anne? The thought pierced my heart, but I pushed it aside and scrambled out of the truck.

"Nice dismount, Grace," Anne said as she smiled at my safe yet clumsy climb down the side of the truck.

"How are they going to do a trial? Who is the judge?"

"Mayor Mueller will be the chief judge, but the council and six citizens they have chosen will be the jury. Ted, of course, has been removed from the proceedings."

"How will it work? I mean does Kenny get a lawyer?"

Anne shrugged. "Buck Fredrickson is going to speak for Kenny from what I understand and Deputy McDaniels is going to act as the prosecutor."

That news made me feel a little better. McDaniels, especially in the state he had kept himself, wouldn't be able to build a good case against anyone. But Buck's involvement didn't sit well with me.

"Buck?" I asked. "Is he really the best choice? I mean, just yesterday he opened fire on a bunch of men on the bridge."

"And he isn't in trouble from the council, is he? He must have showed them why it was in the town's best interest to kill those men."

"Okay, you have a point," I conceded.

People were milling about the library as word had spread of the trial. Ted was standing at the top of the steps talking with several men, including my dad. I waved at him and he waved for me and Anne to come join him.

We worked our way up the steps and waited until the men who would serve as the jury had filed into the building.

"I've saved some seats, we better get in there, it will fill up soon," Ted said as he turned to us.

"Seats?" I asked.

"Come on," Ted said.

When I passed through the doors, I couldn't believe the changes that had been made to the main room of the library. Dozens of chairs had been set up in rows all facing the far end of the building. All of the bookshelves and tables had been moved to the side. I never even imagined they could be moved, although it made sense. They had seemed like permanent fixtures. But with them cleared away, an enormous room was revealed.

At the far end, several long folding tables were set up. One had six chairs sitting behind it. Two other tables were set up facing it. Six chairs were set to the side. That was where the jury would sit.

Behind the tables that were for the prosecution and defense, there was a barricade of library carts. Ted led us up to the third row, where he had saved three seats for us. The building was filling up as people realized they would have to be seated before it began to have any chance of watching what was happening.

Mayor Mueller came out of a door near the head of the room and looked at the table he and the rest of the council would sit behind. He walked behind it and sat down. He looked out toward the crowd and nodded. It apparently met his approval. He walked to the doorway he had appeared from and motioned to the others inside. Soon the entire council had seated themselves behind the long table in the front and the citizen jury had taken their seats along the side of the court.

The seating around us had filled up when the Mayor had appeared and soon there was a commotion near the back of the room.

I turned to see several men furious there didn't seem to be any seats left. Some people were urging the doors be shut, but as warm as it was already in the room, I didn't think that was a good idea.

A series of loud bangs quieted the room and shifted everyone's focus on the mayor. He stood with his gavel in his hand and waited a few seconds for the crowd to settle down.

"This court is now in order. I will hear of no outburst from anyone tonight. Anyone who disturbs this proceeding will be escorted from the building with no warning."

Murmurs started through the crowd and Mayor Mueller again banged the gavel three times.

"We the council and the jury must be able to hear the case. If it becomes impossible to hear, then we will clear the library of all observers. So please, I beg you, just watch and remain silent."

The mayor stood and watched until he was satisfied the low buzz of quiet conversations would not increase in volume.

"Today we are here to determine the fate of Kenneth Jackson in the case of the death of Brent Talley. The prosecution will make its case to the council and jury, then the defense. The prosecution will then be able to make its final plea, and then the defense. After we have heard everything, the council and the jury will meet to make a final decision as to what the verdict is and, if guilty, what the punishment shall be. Let us begin."

From the side door, Kenny, Buck and McDaniels walked into the court and took their seats behind the tables prepared for them. The murmurs started and the mayor banged his gavel and stood up.

Once it had quieted, Mayor Mueller motioned for the deputy to begin speaking.

McDaniels was wearing one of his clean uniforms for a change, and it looked like he had washed and combed his hair for this event.

"Well Mayor Mueller, I didn't have much time to prepare my case, seeing as how Jackson there wanted a speedy trial. But as luck would have it, I don't have much of a case to prepare. We have a confession from Jackson. He gave it willingly and repeatedly. He killed Brent Talley in cold blood, and was found sitting under the dead body early this morning.

"And I might want to remind all of you that he has a long history of criminal activity. He was an admitted thief, he sold and used drugs, he attacked people, he engaged the services of prostitutes and he has served time in jail for the assault of a police officer. Now that the rules of civilization have crumbled, who knows what a man like that is capable of? If we don't end him here, and I want to be perfectly clear that I am talking for his execution, then we will have a lawless killer locked up taking up our precious and hard earned resources.

"There is no use in talking about his guilt, but I do want the council and the jury to think hard about what we should do about those who don't follow what we all understand to be the law. To kill another man, for whatever reason, makes you a murderer. And a murderer cannot be allowed to walk free. And yet, in our current circumstances, we can't afford to keep someone locked up. He should be taken out and killed tonight."

McDaniels gave an awkward small bow toward the table with the council and returned to his seat. He wore a smile that conveyed the idea of smug satisfaction and leaned back in his chair as the mayor gaveled the courtroom back into order.

"He didn't score a single hit," Anne said. "He would have had a better chance if he had just kept his mouth shut."

I agreed, but didn't want to add to the general noise, so I nodded and smiled at her.

When I looked back at the court, Buck had already stood and had moved to the center of the space between the council and the jury. Instead of facing either collection of men and women, however, he turned and faced the audience at the trial.

"Ladies and gentlemen of the council and jury, let there be no mistake, Kenneth Jackson killed Brent Talley and left his body to be found by the whole town. Those facts are not in dispute. However, what we must consider is the type of man Kenny is and why he did what he undeniably did.

"Deputy McDaniels is right about Kenny's past. In fact, I heard about his past in the same place Deputy McDaniels did. Right from the pulpit of the Freewill Baptist Church on the night Kenny was baptized. He told his whole story that night. Confessed his sins against God and man and asked for forgiveness. God forgave him of his past that night, and so did I.

"But his past isn't really what is at issue here. What is at issue is *Quod est necessarium est licitum*, which means what is necessary is lawful. I know the council is familiar with this term as I used it to justify myself and the other men on the Carter's Creek Bridge yesterday. We fired on those who would seek to destroy and dominate us from the outside. Those men would rule us with fear and sow seeds of mistrust and suspicion. That, more than anything, would destroy us and make us slaves to the most powerful man. We would seek him out for protection, hoping that being in his good grace, he would not turn his gaze upon our possessions and our lives.

"And that type of villain is exactly what Brent Talley was. I'm not glad to see him dead, but he was determined to walk down a path of evil. He would take whatever he wanted, without regard for personal privacy or need. He was caught with medicine, tools, jewelry and food. He was sowing the seeds of mistrust and suspicion. He was the barbarian, not at our gates, but living within our midst.

"Kenny saw this danger. Saw it as clearly as you see the danger that no wells, or no latrines, or no food pose to us. He knew it had to be dealt with. He knew if he had waited, others who did not recognize this danger for what it was, would seek to turn their face from the duty that was necessary for our survival.

"Kenny did not run. He did not hide. He was open about what he did and why he did it. He does not seek mercy, he only seeks justice. We are safer with Brent Talley dead and Kenny among us. We are safer with a protector having killed a predator."

Buck turned back to the council, his voice still booming so all in the library could hear him.

"But is that all that is on trial here? Kenny's protection of the town? No. This trial is also about the responsibility we all have to help Kenton survive the current crisis. Kenny has worked the fields. He has helped people create the hand mills we will need when we harvest the wheat and corn. He has dug graves, he has dug wells, and he has put his hand to work where ever it was needed. And late last night, his hand was needed to protect this town from criminals.

"Our only representative of the law enforcement community has shown no interest in protecting us. He has had criminal behavior reported to him and has chosen to ignore the issue. He has spent most of his time five miles from this spot, smoking weed, sleeping with women, and being drunk. He is the arm of the law? No. Kenny is the arm of the law. He saw a need and put his hand to work. He did what needed to be done and I ask the council and the jury to do likewise. If you don't think he should be here, then by all means, send him away. But don't for a minute think any of you will be safer with him gone."

Buck looked out at the audience, shot a withering look at McDaniels, and sat down next to Kenny behind the defendant's table.

The deputy didn't even wait for the mayor to tell him it was his turn. He jumped to his feet and started talking before he had even worked his way from behind his table.

"It don't matter what others may or may not have done, what we are talking about is what Jackson done. He is the one that is on trial here. Not Brent Talley, not me, not anyone else. The facts are he is a dangerous man who has said he will do it again. Now the question we have to ask is do we want a dangerous nigger running about even after he killed someone?"

I didn't gasp audibly at the slur, but I heard several people do so. Racism was still around in Kenton, but it had grown shy in the last couple of decades and wasn't part of acceptable public talk.

To his credit, McDaniels seemed to realize what he had said. His jaw moved but no sound came out for a few seconds.

"My point is, if he breaks the written laws of before and doesn't seem compelled to follow decent civil rules of now, what makes you think he cares about any laws or rules you set for him? He must be punished and we must set an example for others to follow."

The deputy sat back at his table and dropped his head into his hands. I felt a surge of optimism as I thought maybe his case had been blown wide open.

Buck stood and waited until the mayor motioned him forward. There was a commotion that caused the big, burly man to look toward the front door of the library. I turned, with most of the rest of the observers, and saw Lester Collins and several of his men walk in. They were heavily armed, but had the manner of men who were looking for a good time.

"Are we too late?" Lester asked loudly. "I hope the trial ain't over yet."

"What do you want, Collins?" Mayor Mueller asked.

"I just want the opportunity to address the court and all of those in attendance before you go deciding the fate of Kenny, if that would be okay."

Collins moved forward by himself as the mayor nodded.

"Mister Fredrickson was about to make his closing arguments in Kenneth Jackson's defense. You can speak your piece after he is done."

Buck looked back at the mayor and the rest of the council.

"May I continue?" he asked

"Proceed."

"Thank you, Mister Mayor. The case before you today is not about the death of a thief and danger to this town. It is about laws and rights. When we had a robust system of law enforcement, then the laws that had been passed and the system for enforcing those laws made sense.

"But we are in a new world now. When something is stolen from you, it can't be replaced. There is no insurance company that will replace your items. There is no corner store where you can go buy another. There simply isn't anything you can do about your loss. And that means every theft is a permanent set-back for the victim. Every loss of possession is a sliver, or chunk, or major structure out of the victim's life they have built and have no way of getting back.

"Brent Talley was found with medicine among his stolen goods. Medicine that is essential to those who owned it. Was not that a form of murder? Stealing a man's medicine when there was no way to replace it? It was murder and more sinister a version than having a noose put around your neck and hanged for villainy.

"If you find Kenny guilty, then you set the rules of an old society over the welfare of Kenton. You set the dream of what was above the reality of what is. Kenny doesn't deserve death. He doesn't deserve exile. He deserves our respect and admiration for having the strength to do what was needed. Thank you."

The murmurs of the audience surged as Buck sat down. Everyone was whispering their opinions of what the trial meant and what they thought should, and would, happen.

"Order! Order!" Mayor Mueller banged the gavel.

"Now we are going to go meet privately to determine the verdict in this case. Mister Collins, you wanted to address the court before we went into deliberations?"

"Yes, thank you," Lester said. He walked over to the table the council sat at and turned back to the crowded room.

"I just want to say that although Brent Talley was a man who we have had some dealings with, we were unaware of how he procured certain items. It was our understanding he was salvaging from houses of people who no longer needed the amenities he was gathering for us.

"With that in mind, if you have anything missing he may have sold to us, we would be glad to trade it back to you for no more than we gave him. It's only fair.

"As for Kenny here, we understand if you may want to put him to death for his act of violence. If that is indeed the verdict you decide upon, I would be happy to pay a sizable amount of goods and services in order to take him into my compound so we make use of his talents and labor."

Lester bowed and motioned to his men. They turned without a word and forced their way back out of the library. A small wave of space opened in front of Lester as he advanced and within a minute, he was out of sight of where I sat. When I looked back at the court, the council and jury were filing into the side room and Buck was talking with Kenny. They were both smiling. I felt like smiling, too. From what I had seen I thought there was a very good chance Kenny would not be put to death for his actions.

"What do you think, Ted?" Anne leaned across me to ask the appointed leader of our town.

"I don't know," he said. "My gut says Kenny walks, but I have a lot of friendship tied up in that. I'm not sure if I can be objective."

"What about you, David? What do you think Kenny's chances are?" Anne asked.

"I'm not sure," I said. "I think Buck gave a good argument behind the reason Kenny killed him, but I don't know if it was enough to get him out of all trouble. You can't give back a man's life. Killing a man is hard to accept as a good thing."

We chatted and talked about the trial, about what Kenny would have to face based upon all of the possible outcomes, about how this changed the town, how the people in town would now view each other, and what we could expect when crime did happen in the future.

The heat in the room crept up as time went on. The crowd of bodies more than overcame the cool of the evening, and soon everyone was drenched with their own sweat. But no one left. Everyone stayed where they had found a spot, none willing to walk outside and have to hear second-hand the outcome of this evening.

Eventually the door near the front of the court opened and the council and jury came out. They took their seats and the mayor motioned back to the room where they had been shut away. Kenny and Buck came out first. They took their seats at their table and then McDaniels came out. I breathed out in relief as I saw the deputy's jaw clenched and his hands in fists at his sides.

He dropped down in his seat and didn't seem to look at anyone in particular.

Mayor Mueller rose and gaveled the room quiet.

"In the case of Kenneth Jackson, this court has reached a decision."

No one in the room whispered. No one stirred.

"We find that Kenneth Jackson acted in an unlawful manner in the killing of Brent Talley. Therefore, this court has determined that Kenneth Jackson shall be prohibited from entering the township of Kenton for the remainder of his life.

"He will be escorted to the town's limit and the road guards will be instructed to prevent his entrance by any means necessary, up to and including lethal force."

The mayor banged his gavel one more time and the council and jury stood and went back to their room.

Ted sighed as he stood. "Well, better than it could have been, I guess."

Kenny looked back across the few rows of people that separated us and nodded. He wore a frown and I could tell he was disappointed in the verdict. I was relieved he was going to be okay, although I would miss him around town.

The room cleared faster than I would have expected, but with the trial over and the heat in the building making the cool evening a more enjoyable venue for discussion, it made sense.

My dad walked out of the room with Ike and Clint. He spotted me and waved me over.

"I think my dad wants to leave soon," I said to Anne and Ted.

"Take those rides when you can, talk to you tomorrow, David," Ted said.

"I'll be over tomorrow night for dinner," Anne added. "Let your folks know."

I said my goodbyes and made my way over to my dad.

"How are you?" I asked. He looked very pale and seemed short of breath.

"I'm fine. Would just like to get out of this suit and sit in a cool bath tub."

"When we get home, I'll go get you water," I said.

He smiled and patted me on the shoulder. "Sounds good, David. Let step outside and see if we can't find a cool breeze."

We left the library and stepped out into the night. I almost shivered as we crossed the threshold of the front doors, the change in temperature was that drastic. Dad needed to hold onto my arm as we walked down the steps. I had never seen him this weak and I just wanted to get him home and cooled down.

Clint was already in the truck and waiting for us. There would be no collection of kids and dogs with darkness already covering the town. Clint turned the lights on as we approached the vehicle. The dim headlights blazed like the noon-day sun as they cut through the darkness of the tree shaded square.

I helped Dad into the cab and scrambled into the back as Clint started the engine. A running vehicle was still enough of an oddity that we attracted a fair crowd who waved and smiled as we pulled away from the square.

A few seconds later, the truck was running down Granger road. I raised my head above the roof of the truck cab, fully prepared to take an insect or two in my face, just to feel the cold rush of the wind.

The night was still moonless, and a thin wispy layer of clouds blocked all but the brightest stars from shining down into the darkness. I knew why the dark scared us. I knew why primitive man was drawn to the light of the fire. Twin beams of pure white light ran before me, driving the darkness back. That light meant safety, it meant no fear of the unknown.

We arrived at the house and I hopped out of the back of the truck. What was a risk just a few hours before seemed like the most natural thing to do as the ride energized me. Kenny was safe, the darkness was vanquished, and I was home.

EIGHTTEEN

The final drop of solder was in place. I blew on it, more out of habit than to cool it, as I took it back inside. I had a small steel fire pit out back that I burned charcoal in and heated up an old wood-burning blade. I found that was a perfect setup to melt solder as I tried to piece together parts of the short-wave radio I had spent the last two months working on.

"Good luck," Dad said. He was reading a magazine while sitting at the table. I didn't believe there is a single magazine in town that he hadn't read. Maybe not the ones in Luke's collection, but then again, maybe he liked them for the articles.

"Eighty-fifth time's the charm," I said as I headed back to my room. Every time I would think I had it figured out, I would find another spot on a board that had burned out, or a component that had cracked.

I slid the small green chip into the back of the radio. I attached the copper lead that would connect the receiver to the power regulator, and then I clipped on the power supply. I made sure the connections to the battery were solid and I pushed the switch to the on position.

The dials moved, the lights popped on, and then miraculously, stayed on.

I couldn't believe it. It looked live and wasn't making a hiss or sputtering.

I reached out with great care and moved the frequency dial. Healthy static came from the speakers as I moved the dial.

Then I heard it. The broken pattern of a received signal. Far too faint to clearly hear, it was a signal being broadcast from another radio.

I turned off the radio and paced around the room. I shook from excitement and fear. Then I turned the radio back on. The broken signal was still there. I had fixed the radio.

I turned the short-wave off again and carefully packed it in my gym bag. It was no longer in the compact form that would fit snugly in the case it was bought in. I knew how each component fit together, though, so I packed it so it would be safe as I carried it out to Ted's place and the cell tower.

"What's wrong, dear?" Mom asked as I emerged from the hallway.

"I got it," I said. As much as I was trying to remain calm I could tell the excitement was building.

"The radio?" Dad asked. He stood up from the table and looked at me with wide eyes. A smiled crept across his face.

"The radio," I said as I smiled back. "I have to get to Ted's so we can set it up."

"You did it, David," he said. "You may have saved us all. I'm so proud of you, son."

"Thanks, Dad," I said. "I might be gone for a while, but I'll fill you in on all the details when I get back."

I left the house and shut the front door behind me. I wanted to run all the way through town and up the north road to Ted's house, but I made myself walk. The last thing I wanted to do was trip and damage the cargo I had packed so carefully.

The sun was drifting toward noon. Tendrils of smoke in the distance showed signs some of the raiders to the west were still active. As I passed the wheat fields, I saw several of the older farmers with long handled scythes showing some of the younger men how to swing the hand tools in the most efficient manner. The wheat was just a few days from being ready to harvest, as long as the rains held off.

There were certain landmarks the town had unconsciously established, and a major one was the first wheat harvest. With enough wheat to turn into flour, we could have bread again. While the meat and vegetable diet was starting to feel right, having a slice of bread with dinner or a biscuit with breakfast would be marvelous.

I made my way past Miller Street. A crowd of women and children were gathered outside Millie Marsh's house. One of the kids would bring my parents their evening meal when I didn't show up. I wanted to go over there and share my good news, but I thought I should make sure the radio worked at the tower before I talked about it. The early July sun was hot and the air was humid as I made my way past the town square and headed for the highway out of town. The armed men at the north barricade waved at me. I just waved back and kept my pace. They must have sensed I was in a hurry, as they didn't try to stop me to talk.

It was just three miles from the north edge of town to the gate of Ted's compound. The blacktop turn off was a mile away, and then there were two high hills in the next two miles. A few months ago I would have been winded by the four relatively flat miles from my folk's house to the library, but now my legs were still loose and responsive as I passed the barricade with the armed guards. I didn't go to the compound often, but they knew I had been there a couple of times. They yelled to me to say hello to Kenny when I saw him. Kenny had made some very vocal allies among several of the men who saw themselves as protectors of Kenton.

The hills proved no problem as I scurried my way along the blacktop. My feet wanted to run, but I had to make sure the radio arrived in good condition. Finally, I turned into the long drive heading to the gates. Kenny was clearing some brush along the side of the road.

"David," he called. "What are you doing up here this morning?"

"I got it," I said.

Kenny slipped his machete in its sheath. His eyes widened and he let out a loud whoop.

"Let's get you inside," he said. "Tom! Tom! Come here!"

I followed Kenny into the compound with my precious cargo. Tom came running up to meet Kenny, who danced around me like a dog happy to see his owner back from the grocery store.

"What is it?" Tom asked. "The radio?" He was staring at the gym bag I held carefully in front of me.

I nodded and Tom darted off toward the small shed where he had prepared the space for the radio to sit.

He had the door open and motioned me inside as I kept the fast walking pace I had established since I stepped out of my front door. I entered the room and set the gym bag on the table. I unzipped the bag and carefully removed the packed radio. It looked like it was all intact.

I attached the battery and turned the power on. Lights glowed and dials moved.

Tom and Kenny stared at it for a solid minute as I moved everything off the table and motioned to Tom.

"Go ahead, set it up to the antennae," I said.

Tom nodded and attached the coaxial cable to the radio. The choppy signal wavered and then stabilized. I adjusted the frequency dial and we heard a voice.

"Roger Charlie 4. We had you set. Over."

"We'll be heading up to next point in a few. Contact when we get there. Charlie 4 out."

I picked up the hand mic and prayed it would work. I was amazed just to hear voices coming in over the radio, to not be able to talk back to them would be such a disappointment.

"Hello," I said. "Can anyone hear me?"

For a few seconds, the three of us waited as we only heard the inert static of a solid signal.

"Who is this?" a voice crackled back.

"My name is David and I am from Kenton. We just got our radio working."

A few more seconds went by before we got another response.

"David from Kenton, it's good to hear from you. And congratulations on repairing your radio. That couldn't have been easy. What is your general situation?"

"Don't give away too much information," Kenny said. "We don't know who he is or where he is."

I nodded. That made sense and I knew I needed to be brief and terse.

"We are doing fine," I said. "Who are you and where are you located."

"I am Sergeant Webb and I am sitting in a bunker in Missouri. Where is Kenton located?"

"He's trying to get you to give up our position. He isn't giving his up," Kenny said.

"Be careful, David, but we can't give in to paranoia," Tom said.

"We are pretty close, I think. How is the situation where you are?" I asked.

"We have control of the general area. Have you had trouble with outside people?"

"A few," I said. "We were able to make sure we weren't bothered by them."

"I pulled a map up, David. Looks like you are about 90 miles from us. We are in Cape Girardeau."

"Who is we, if you don't mind me asking?"

"U.S. Army Reserve unit from town. We had some equipment survive the burst, and we acted quickly to establish control and mobilize the population. How did Kenton go about setting themselves up?

"We were able to organize quickly. Got wells and latrines set up, started planting crops in the first few days."

"Hold on, David from Kenton. I'll just be a minute."

"What do you think that is about?" I asked Tom and Kenny.

"Not sure," said Tom. "But we should be taking notes."

"Do you think they can pinpoint where we are broadcasting from?" Kenny asked.

"I'm not sure," Tom said. "But they already know where Kenton is."

"David? Are you there?" Sergeant Webb said over the radio.

"I'm here, Sergeant."

"Okay, is there anything you need up there? We don't have much food but we can come and try to help you with water purification."

I looked at Kenny and Tom. I was hoping they would have an idea of what to ask for, but they looked back at me with the same look I thought I had.

"Medicine," I said finally. "There are quite a few folks running low on medicine."

"Yeah, that's something we are all dealing with. Can't help you there. Listen, how this normally works is, we send a team out to assess the situation of people calling for help. But you sound like you have everything under control. Is that what I am understanding?"

"It's pretty well under control. It's been tough, but I think the town will be okay."

"I know it may be a lot to ask, but how many folks do you have up there."

Kenny smacked me on the shoulder and emphatically shook his head "No."

"Prudence would be to let that question lie for the time being, Sergeant."

"Understood. We would like to maintain contact with you, David. Are you in charge of the radio?"

"Uh, no. Actually, I fixed it and we are just trying it now. Tom is with me and he will be the one who mans the radio for us."

I handed the mic to Tom. It was a thrill to speak to someone else from a far location, but Tom was who would be running our communications station.

"Thank you, David," he said as I stood from the chair. He sat down and turned the mic back on.

Wilson Harp   EMP

"This is Tom," he said. "I have some questions about what is going on if you don't mind."

Kenny tapped me on the shoulder and motioned for me to follow him as he walked out of the small shed.

I left the shed and closed the door behind me.

"Wow, man. I just can't believe it," he said. "David, you have reconnected us with the outside world. And whether it is better or worse out there, we will at least know."

"We will." I said. I realized my hands were shaking and I still wanted to run. It was sinking in that I had done it. I had fixed the radio. The frontier around Kenton was no longer limited to the range of Buck and his hunters. It was miles and miles away, days by foot. If the army really did have control of Cape Girardeau, then we had access to the Mississippi river and Illinois. If we had access to Illinois, then I could make my way to Chicago.

"You okay?" Kenny asked.

"Yeah, just all catching up to me."

"Well let's go tell Sophia and the others. They'll want to know. You can hang out here until Ted gets back this evening. He'll know who to tell, and when, in town."

"Sounds good to me," I said. "I feel a little shaky now, anyway. What time is it?"

Kenny looked up at the sky. "Looks like it's right at noon. Let's go kill a couple of hours."

We walked down the path to Sophia's house. The gardens showed abundant crops. Cucumbers, melons, squash, tomato plants, small hot pepper bushes and neat rows of cabbages, were all proof Ted and his people would be well-fed come winter time.

"They will be harvesting the wheat in the next few days," I told Kenny. "Looks like we might get some flour within a few weeks."

"I bet you are missing bread, aren't you?"

"You aren't?" I asked.

He smiled and shook his head. "Nah, Sophia had laid in about two hundred pounds of flour before the event. She had it sealed up in big tubs. That was her 'end of the world' supplies. Ted doesn't want word to get out about how much we have up here, but we won't be hurting for flour for a couple of years. Hopefully by that time things will be better and flour won't be a concern."

My mouth watered at the thought of a piece of bread. "Do you think... I mean if it isn't too much to ask?"

Kenny smiled at me. "You fixed the radio. I'm going to fix you whatever you want for lunch."

We entered Sophia's house and were met by their two large golden retrievers. I reached down to pet them and marveled at how well fed and fit they seemed.

Sophia came out of the kitchen with her daughter Kaylee in tow.

"David, what a nice surprise. I didn't think we were going to be having visitors today." She glanced at Kenny as if it was his fault she wasn't prepared to entertain guests.

"We have a radio, Sophie," Kenny said.

"We do? David, did you get it?" She squealed bringing her other two kids running into the room.

"Where is it? Is it set up already?" she asked.

"Yeah, Tom's talking to—"

I was interrupted as she threw herself on me. She hugged me and held me tight as I tried to tell her who Tom was talking to.

"Hey sis, I think David's hungry. What can you make him?"

Sophia let me go and spun around hugging her kids. "Lunch. We'll fix lunch. Is there anything special I can make for you?" Tears were running down her cheeks as she laughed and jumped with her kids. Even the dogs joined in to the happy sounds and movements.

"Whatever you were planning will be fine," I said.

She stopped and looked at me as she wiped her eyes. "Okay, but I want to make something special for this occasion."

"Chocolate chip cookies." The words fell out of my mouth without thinking.

"Yeah, mom. Chocolate chip cookies," her kids repeated.

"Okay," she said. "I still have some chips. I'll make you a batch."

"Can I maybe take a couple home with me? They're my dad's favorite."

"Absolutely," Sophia said. "I'll make some we can eat tonight in celebration and then I will give you some to take to your family. Just don't let word get out. I can't bake cookies for the whole town."

I smiled and found a seat in her living room as she, the kids and the dogs all paraded into the kitchen.

"You have that much of a craving for chocolate chip cookies?" Kenny asked as he sat down in a large leather chair.

"I would love one," I said. "But really, it's about my dad. When this all started, we talked about what we would want. I wanted to go home to Chicago, find Lexi and Emma, and figure out how and where we were going to live. His goals were simpler. He wanted to ride in a car again and feel the wind whip by. He wanted to have a reason to get dressed up. And, he wanted a chocolate chip cookie. He had the first two a couple of weeks ago at your trial, now I'll be able to make all of his wishes come true."

"That's nice," Kenny said. "I get that. Sometimes we dream so big it's better to focus on other people's dreams. It makes us think if we can help them along the way, then maybe someone else will come along and help us. When I was leaving New Orleans, I was stuck in Shreveport for a week or so. No money, no food, no place to sleep. But, I had a friend up in Memphis, so I just needed a ride. Took me two days, but then this guy just walked up to me and said 'Hey, you look like you don't belong. I'm heading out of town. Want a ride?' I almost turned him down, but he held out a bag of burgers to me and I figured if he was crazy enough to feed me and trust me in his car, I would leave Shreveport with him."

"Where was he heading?"

"Memphis. He told me he was going up there to tell his church what he saw down in New Orleans. They were going to buy supplies and then go down to help with the clean-up. My friend lived two blocks from his church. He gave me a ride, but to me that meant a chance at life. And I think it meant more for him, too. You are going to give your dad a cookie, but it means a dream fulfilled, and that's powerful, David."

"Dream fulfillment one cookie at a time," I said.

"Powerful."

I didn't feel powerful, but his words showed me sometimes what I do resonates louder than I realize. I don't get to see all of the effects because I am in the center. The radio was my big excuse for not going to get Lexi and Emma. Now the path was clear. I needed to think about my own wishes. And with all of dad's wishes completed, mine somehow did seem more achievable. Powerful indeed.

A short while later, I sat down for a meal I would not have passed up before the event. Baked chicken with a honey and thyme glaze, carrots, green beans with bacon drippings, and water sweetened with berries. Sophia set down a small basket of drop biscuits and my mouth watered so much I feared I would drool.

We sat around the table and talked about anything and everything. The children drove the topics of conversation. They were mostly interested in their animals and when they would have more visitors. Soon, though, Sophia set them to their chores and Kenny and I sat and nibbled at the ends of the luncheon.

"Kenny." The front door eased open as Ted called.

"In here Ted," Kenny responded.

"Baked chicken. Any left?" Ted asked as he came in.

"Nah, David here took your portion."

"He deserves it, getting that radio up and going. Good job," Ted said as he walked over and sat beside me. "I was just speaking with Tom, he is getting a pretty clear picture of the situation."

"How's it look?" asked Kenny.

"Not good. The major cities are inaccessible and most places weren't able to pull it together quick enough to fend off disease."

"How much of the world was hit?" I asked.

"As far as our army friends can tell, all of it. There might have been some remote places that didn't feel the sting, but they wouldn't have had much to fry out in the first place."

"So this is it? This is the starting point of rebuilding our world?" I asked.

"Yes. Kind of," said Ted. "We do have books and knowledge of technologies, so it is reasonable to believe we can quickly move ourselves forward."

"And you have to realize, David," Kenny added. "Not everyone was affected. The Amish, for example, probably aren't living too different. Low technology nations and people in remote areas may have had some luxuries taken, but their essential day to day life goes on as normal."

"That's true, I guess. I just can't imagine how all areas will get everything they need to rebuild civilization," I said.

"At least for the next several decades. Local areas will need to specialize and then trade will start again. Routes will have to be secured and kept safe. As that happens, and as laws develop, people will resettle lands that have been polluted," Ted said.

"Polluted?" I asked. "How so?"

"Well, unless I'm mistaken, there were thousands of meltdowns at nuclear power plants all around the world. Most of them probably were localized. Radioactive dust probably created a kill zone of ten to fifteen miles downwind of them, but for the most part, we just need to avoid those areas for a couple of decades. After a time, people can start going in for short periods and recover materials."

I had never thought of nuclear plants. Were there nuclear plants on the way to Chicago? I would need maps and more information. Maybe it was for the best I didn't head up right away.

"What about the cities?" Kenny asked. "I mean, I figure cholera hit pretty fast, but do they know what the cities look like? Did they all burn?"

"Not sure," Ted said. "If they have some transport, they may have had a look at Memphis or Saint Louis, but I don't know if Tom has been specific with his questions yet."

"Are you staying for dinner, David?" Sophia asked from the kitchen door.

"Oh, no. I should probably head back."

"Cookies aren't done yet, but they are about to go in the oven. You are welcome to stay if you want," she said.

"Stay, David," Ted told me. "I saw Anne and she said she would keep your parents company tonight. She knew it might take some time up here and if everything didn't go right, you might not make it back this evening."

"Okay," I said. "If Anne is keeping an eye on them, I'll stay for dinner."

"Stay the night," Sophia said from the kitchen. "Kenny will set up a room for you. Bet you would like a hot shower tomorrow."

"You have water pressure for a shower?" I asked.

"Enjoy Shangri-La, David," Ted said. "A night in paradise."

NINETEEN

"David!"

I sat straight up. I wasn't where I was supposed to be.

"David!"

The voice was insistent. A door opened. Not from where I expected. Why was Lexi yelling? No, it wasn't Lexi.

"David, get up. Now."

Anne was framed in the doorway, a light silhouetted her.

"What?" I asked. I was sure my voice sounded feeble and confused, because it was.

"David, get up," she repeated.

"Come on, grab your pants and put them on." I heard Kenny behind her.

I swung my legs over the side of the bed. The bed in Kenny's house. I had stayed up at Ted's compound because Anne…

"Aren't you supposed to be with my folks?" I asked Anne as she tossed me my t-shirt from a chair.

"Get dressed," she said. "You have to get dressed."

Her voice was strained and I saw her eyes were red and puffy.

"What's wrong?" I asked. I was alert and aware. My senses were sharp and my movements efficient as I pulled on my pants and located my boots. I had slipped my t-shirt on and had my boots in my hand before she spoke again.

"Ride Bonnie, and get home David. You just need to get home."

She was calm, but rattled. I could tell something terrible had happened, but I also knew I would get no more information out of her.

When my feet were firmly planted in my boots, I hurried out of Kenny's house. The room that had been set up for me had no windows, but as I moved out of the glow of the lantern Kenny held, I noticed the pre-dawn light was already wakening the world.

I left his front door and almost ran into Bonnie. She was saddled and ready to go, so I mounted her in one smooth motion and guided her toward the gate. She sensed my unease and by the time we hit the driveway, we were at a trot. When her hooves hit the blacktop, I urged her to run. We were at a full gallop once we hit the highway. I knew Anne would have to check her hooves later, but at the moment I just needed to get home.

I raced past the checkpoint, the men there calling to me. I had the stray thought they might shoot at me since I didn't heed their call. But as there was no sharp report that crackled through the morning stillness and I didn't topple from Bonnie, I assumed they recognized me and let my wild passage go unimpeded.

Through the town Bonnie galloped. More people were up and about than I would have figured, but I normally didn't head into town this early. It wasn't so crowded I had to hold my mount back, though. I pushed ahead and rode hard. If Anne had mounted up and sought me out this early, and if she wouldn't tell me what the problem was…

I pushed forward even more. Bonnie had foam flecking at her mouth and her flanks were getting wet. I was running her harder than she had probably been ridden in years, if ever.

I saw my parent's house and I saw the small group of people on the front lawn. Then I saw Luke. He stepped out of the house and I could see his head bobbing, as if he was crying. Someone in the group had seen or heard Bonnie racing down the road. They turned as one, and I saw Luke hold up his hand in the light mist of the morning.

I pointed Bonnie toward the house and pulled her up as her hoof hit the front lawn. I jumped from the saddle and ran the last 15 feet or so.

"David," Luke said. "I'm so sorry."

I pushed past him and saw my mother sitting on the couch with Rose. I froze. I knew something bad had happened when Anne woke me, but I didn't want to think about who it was. I felt like someone was squeezing my heart. I turned and ran down the hall. I looked in their room. Their room. My mom and dad's room. There in the room that I didn't belong. There was my dad, sleeping in the middle of the bed. Sleeping. But he never slept on his back and he never slept in the middle. The sheets were neatly tucked around him.

"David, I'm so sorry," Luke said softly from behind me.

"When? Did he… Was I too late?"

"He was gone when your mom woke. Anne tore out of here to get you, but by then… I'm so sorry David. He passed in his sleep."

I felt Luke's arm around me. I realized my legs were weak and I shouldn't be standing, but Luke was holding me up.

"Let's go to your mother," he said.

I tore my eyes away from my dad and nodded. I kept my eyes closed as we went to the living room. I never wanted to see the house again. Its image was a mockery of my life. The place where I had grown up. It couldn't be the place I saw my dad dead.

I sat on the couch and found my mother had her arms around me.

I wanted to say something comforting to her. I wanted to remind her he was a good father, husband and man. That I loved him and he loved me and her. I wanted to express my love for him, my love for her, and my sorrow for her.

I couldn't. All I could do was sob and hold her. She did the same. No words of comfort, no words of grief came from her. Just tears and her arms.

I opened my eyes and saw her. Her face was contorted in pain, her grief mirrored mine. I blinked away the tears and saw there were others in the room. They whispered and spoke. I heard a few people in the kitchen.

Luke and another man walked out of the hallway and crossed the living room to me and my mother.

"Abbey, David. We need to get Pat ready for burial," Luke said softly. His eyes still brimmed with tears. I knew how much he loved my dad.

Mom sobbed harder as Luke told us what we both knew.

"What should we bury him in?" Luke asked me. Mom was too far gone to make a decision.

"His suit," I said. "He would want to be buried in his suit."

My voice cracked and I felt weak. The light coming through the windows was no longer the low golden light of morning, but was now the clear white light of noon. My stomach growled. I wondered how long I had been sitting with Mom.

"Here, try to eat," Rose said to Mom as she approached with a bowl of soup. "You need to eat."

Mom let go of me and wiped her eyes. "I'm so sorry, David," she whispered.

"I'm sorry, Mom," I said back. "I don't know what to do or say."

"Neither do I," she said. "I will never know what to do again."

I knew what she meant. More than the EMP, my world was different because of this. I could always rely on my dad. He was always there if I needed him. I didn't realize how much I just needed him to be there.

Mom took the offered bowl of soup and sipped some from the spoon. Sarah handed me a bowl.

"I'm sorry about Pat," she said. "I wish it hadn't happened."

"Thank you," I said. "I wish none of this had happened. If it hadn't, you would be home with your family and I would be home with mine. Dad wouldn't have run out of pills and he could have been going to his cardiologist."

"But it did happen, David. If my mom and dad had picked me up after their cruise and I got back home with my friends. I would have complained about being stuck here for spring break."

She reminded me so much of Emma. I hugged her to me and she hugged me back.

"But," she continued. "I would never have realized how much I loved grandma and grandpa. And how much they loved me."

I looked at her and realized she was trying to comfort me. She realized I needed help seeing the situation for what it was. I was heart-broken like I had never been, and I needed help to see it.

"What about your parents, honey?"

"They were on a ship in the middle of the ocean. They have to be dead by now."

I broke. My tears flowed like rivers and I wailed as my grief, my fear, and what I knew as the truth all came rushing in on me at once.

It was some time later I realized I had been holding my mom again. She whispered words of comfort to me as she kissed my forehead.

I sensed a change in the room and looked up to see Ted and Anne sitting at the kitchen table. They just watched me suffer in my grief. Then I heard the noise from the back of the house and Luke walked out of the hallway.

"He is ready," he said. "We are going to take him soon. David, would you like to say goodbye?"

I nodded and hugged Mom hard. Then I stood on shaky legs. I glanced over at Ted and Anne. I gave them a tight smile and started toward the bedroom. My head whipped back as I recognized my gym bag on the table.

I stepped over to the table and opened the bag. There was what I hoped to see. A small plastic container Sophia had given me after dinner the night before. I opened it and looked inside. Three of the four chocolate chip cookies had broken on the trip down from the compound. I wasn't sure which of my friends had carried the bag back to me, but I owed them a lot at that moment. I lifted the unbroken cookie and carried it reverently to my dad. This was my final gift to him and the fulfillment of his wish.

I entered his room and saw him lying on the bed. The sheet that would be his burial shroud was under his body. His feet were bare. That was a tradition the people of Kenton had continued. I approached him and looked on his face. It was a familiar face, but not the one I had seen the day before. This face was a mockery of life, a sad parody of the man I loved. I had never considered how much love and care funeral directors took to make sure that the body in the coffin looked like it was just resting. Dad had been dead for just a few hours and he looked dead.

I lifted the side of his suit jacket and tucked the chocolate chip cookie into its pocket. Then I placed it back.

"Sorry, Dad," I said. "I was a day late with your cookie. I love you and I hope you know that. And I know you were proud of me, and that was what I hoped for more than anything in this life. I will take care of Mom for you. And I'll see you soon. Pray for me where you are and watch out for me if you can. But most of all, enjoy your rest and your reward. If anyone earned it, you did."

I looked on my father's face one last time and turned to leave the room. Luke and my mother stood in the doorway. I went and hugged my mother. She hugged me back and I could sense a peace around her as I pulled out of the hug.

"He was proud of you, David. And so am I," she said.

I nodded to Luke and went down the hall. Anne and Ted stood near the dining room table.

"I'm so sorry, David. If I had known, I would have had you return last night," Ted said.

"It's okay," I replied. "I knew it was coming. We all did. He had kept cutting back on his medication and last week he was finally out. I… I just can't believe it's come to this. We are all going to die because we aren't smart enough to figure out how to live."

Anne shook her head. "No David, we are all going to die because that is what life is. We need to live life until we die. There is no other way."

I nodded as I thought about what she said. Was I living life or was I just marking time? Death was coming and I had no way to avoid that meeting.

"You should know Tom got some good news from the men at Cape," Ted said. "They are going to send a team here eventually to provide us with things. They were impressed by what we had done. They are going to let us stay as we are because they want our input on how to get other towns to work as well as we have."

"That's wonderful, Ted. How soon before they arrive and what will they bring?"

"I don't know. The wheat harvest starts tomorrow, so we will have flour soon. Beyond that, the only thing we really need is a steady supply of milk. Maybe they will bring some milk cows with them. In any case, it was men like your father who stayed clear headed, understood the situation, and then acted to solve it that has helped us survive. He was a hero."

"Thank you," I said.

Anne motioned behind me and I turned to see my mom walking toward me. She had a smile on her face and tears on her cheeks.

I went to her and wrapped my arms around her.

"He went ahead to get everything ready for me," she said. "He always said he would take care of me, and he has. He has left me with you as he gets everything ready. I didn't expect it, but I now know what waits for me when I leave."

I hugged her tighter and kissed her cheek. I felt empty and drained, but somehow lighter. I didn't know what to do, so I just kept hold of my mother.

Luke motioned for two other men to follow him back to where my dad rested. I guided Mom over to the couch and sat with her. We watched as three men carried the sheet wrapped figure of my father out of the front door of our house. We stood and waited until we heard them tell the wagon to start.

"Do you think you can walk to the graveyard, Mom?" I asked.

She nodded. "I can do this for him. I expected him to do it for me. I know I have the Alzheimer's. I was so mad at him for trying to get me to take the medicine, you know?"

I helped Mom stand and we walked out the front door. Clyde was pulling the wagon, like he had so many times these last few months. He knew from the sense of people around him where he was going and what he was pulling behind him. His head was up, but he had a calm, measured pace. I was afraid Mom would fall behind, but her pace seemed firm and sure.

"I don't want you to hate me, David," Mom said. "I think I may have caused this. Your dad worried about me so much, and I think my… erratic behavior caused him more stress."

"It wasn't your fault, Mom. He had a heart condition. If you hadn't made him go to the doctor to get it checked years ago, he wouldn't have discovered it."

"That's sweet of you, dear. But I know how bad I can get. At least I think I do. At first, I watched my bad days like I was locked in a room watching through a window. I saw how forgetful and emotional I was, but I couldn't do anything about it. Now that window is less clear and I don't remember all the things I do. I'm getting worse and I know Pat suffered from watching. I just want you to know how much I appreciated and loved him for all he put up with."

"He knew, Mom. He did. And I promised him I would take care of you, so you should know I appreciate and love you and will help you as best as I can."

Mom squeezed my hand and stopped walking. I looked at her and tears started rolling down her cheeks again.

"Thank you. I don't know that I can do this on my own."

TWENTY

It was a warm morning when they finally arrived. The calendar said it was late September, but the summer still had a firm grip on the land. I was in the field checking on the tomatoes when I heard the bell in town ring. I slipped the small clippers into my belt and headed toward town. Most of the others in the field headed away from their work as well. The bell meant something big, so we could afford a break from a few hours of work in the hot sun to see what was happening. As I got closer to the town center, I could hear the noise of excited people and something else. I realized it was the rumble of vehicles. Not just a couple of tractors or a car or two, but many, large vehicles.

The sound of the engines spurred me to walk faster and soon I could see the source of the excitement and sound. Six military vehicles, green and well maintained, idled near the square. Dozens of men in uniform, weapons in hands, stood around them.

Ted and Mayor Mueller talked with a large soldier who wore a heavy jacket in spite of the heat. He wore a black beret and wrote on a piece of paper attached to a clip board. Several soldiers had formed a loose perimeter around the men and a crowd was starting to form along that line.

One of the soldiers pointed at me and handed his rifle to the soldier next to him. He took off his helmet and pushed his way through the crowd.

"David!" he said.

"Frank?"

I couldn't believe it. Frank Anderson had not only survived, he had made it back to Kenton.

We hugged in the middle of the street. Frank looked around and started picking out people in the crowd he knew.

"I was going to keep quiet and to myself," he said. "I wasn't sure who would be here or if I would recognize home."

"It's good to see you. I can't believe you made it back."

"Yeah, it feels weird. I mean, I heard Wilcox wasn't in good shape, and that's where my apartment was. So I guess this little town really is home."

"So you're staying?"

"Captain Davidson wants to leave some men here, so he thought it might be a good idea to include someone with local roots. My folks may be gone, but I do know quite a few people in town. Or at least I hope I do. How bad has it been?"

"Population swelled to about six thousand right at the beginning. We have about four thousand now."

"That's actually really good, David. Most places are under a third. Those that are alive at all. Any locals holding out on their own?"

"Ted Riggins," I pointed to my friend. "He has about a dozen people up at his place. They are well situated and don't really need any help. Lester Collins has about forty at his place they seem fine as well."

Frank nodded as he looked around. "No riots recently?"

"No riots ever. Ted took control on the first day and he established a council including the mayor."

"The captain will be pleased. I haven't been in a town without riots. Kenton seems to be a gem of a town."

"How long will they be here?" I asked. "What can they do to help us?"

"Well, not too much, honestly. Bring law and order, but ya'll need it less than most. We'll set you up with a telegraph which will allow you to communicate with other settlements. We'll patrol roads out of here which should open some travel and trade."

"What about milk cows? That is the big thing we are missing,"

Frank scratched his chin. "Rare. There might be some we could bring in, but it would likely be for trade."

"What could we trade?"

"About anything. Kenton is in really good shape. I wouldn't be surprised if the captain doesn't send some refugees to you."

"David," Anne called to me as she came across the square.

I motioned her to join me and Frank.

"Anne Franklin?" he asked. "Are you two…?"

"No," I said. "I'm married, remember?"

He shrugged and waved at her as she approached.

"Oh my goodness, Frank!" she cried as she recognized him.

"Anne, good to see you again."

"How did you end up in the army?"

"They were looking for bodies to fill uniforms and I was in the right place at the right time."

"You looked like you had some news, Anne," I said.

"Yes. The Captain told Ted and the mayor they have secured the road all the way to Cape and have a solid hold on both sides of the bridge."

"Really?" I asked. "Is that true, Frank?"

"Yeah, only known bridge that's safe to cross from Saint Louis to Memphis. Why? Were you planning on heading across?"

"Eventually," I said.

"Why?" Frank asked.

"His wife and daughter are up in Chicago, Frank."

Frank turned his face away and swore under his breath. "You need to take a trip to Cape, David. You need to see what even a small city is like. Maybe Lexi and Allie got lucky."

"Emma," I corrected.

"Sorry. Emma. Maybe they got lucky, but… you said eventually. So something is keeping you here?"

He shot a glance at Anne. She noticed and squirmed.

"My mom," I said. "She is struggling with her Alzheimer's. She needs me here."

"What about your dad?"

"July. Same day as radio contact with Cape."

"Oh no, David. I'm so sorry. Pat was a great man."

"Thanks," I said. "But with him gone, I will stay with Mom. I have to keep hope I can find Lexi and Emma, but I have to be realistic as well. They are probably gone, but Mom is alive and needs someone to stay with her. After… well, afterward, we will see what I can do."

"Okay, David," Frank said. "I need to get back to my unit and find out what we will be doing here. We will likely be here a few days taking inventory and getting a census built up."

"Great to see you, Frank," I said. "I'm glad you're okay. We'll talk more tonight, but I got to get back to the south fields."

"I understand, until tonight."

Frank went back to his unit. Anne and I looked at the men in uniform as they set up a few tents. Ted and Mayor Mueller led their officers into the library. I'm sure they would want to see our maps, figure out the food situation, and ask questions about our security.

"Is today the day that everything changes?" Anne asked me.

"No," I said. "It is a big day, though. Contact with the outside world is now more than just what Ted says Tom has been told. I can't wait to hear what Frank has to say. I'm sure it will terrify me, but at the same time, anything outside of Kenton has seemed surreal. Maybe I'll be able to start realizing how bad it has been for the others."

Anne squinted into the noon-day sun. "It's getting late. You need an extra helper in the south fields?"

"Sure, we can always use extra help. Usually you don't volunteer for things like that."

She shrugged. "Just want to talk, you know? You are a pretty good person to talk to, David. I want to go with you when you head to Chicago. You know that."

"Yeah, when it comes time, you can go with me."

"Good."

"What do you think it will mean now the military will secure trade lines?" I asked.

"Besides more trade?" she asked back with a smile. "Probably more news and meeting new people."

"Probably. It's amazing how much such little news can become the talk of the day."

"Yeah. The wedding last week brought the town to a stop," she said. "Not the deaths, though. No one wants to talk about the deaths."

"People need hope, Anne. Weddings, pregnancies, and births give us that hope."

"Lester has five pregnant girls up at his place."

"Booze and lack of self-control tends to do that. He has plenty of resources, let him use up a little more. We don't have say over his people and they don't bother us in town."

"I don't like it, but that's the way it needs to be, I guess."

I turned and started walking toward the south field. Anne walked alongside me.

"That is the future for Collins and his group. Weed, booze, sex and enough guns to hold it all. Ted's place will outshine them eventually, but both groups will thrive."

"What about Kenton, David?"

"It's a farm town that never quite lost its roots. The land and the soil have provided food, clothing and shelter for poor people for generations. It will provide for generations more."

"And what about you, David? What do you have?"

"Work to do," I said with a smile. "Work and a place to rest. People that care about me and people that depend on me. I guess that's all I really need. It's all I've ever really had. I think it's all most people ever have, if they are lucky."

Anne walked beside me and we worked in the field until near sundown. We gathered dinner from Millie for Mom, and Anne joined us for dinner that night.

Tomorrow I would work in the fields again.

NOTE FROM THE AUTHOR

Thank you for reading the story of David Hartsman and his story of survival in the aftermath of a global EMP. I often wonder what I would do in certain events or how I would react to different situations. In the case of a huge event like an EMP, the uncertainty of life would surely throw different twists each day and would constantly challenge our beliefs and convictions.

My hope is that you were entertained by this book and that you will look for my other works to entertain you as well. If you liked this story, I invite you to leave a review where you purchased it. If you would like to sign up for e-mail notifications of my new releases, please visit my website at www.wilsonharpbooks.com.

Thank you
Wilson Harp

Bright Horizons

Earth has made first contact with an alien race. At the historic first meeting, an ambush put peace for humanity out of reach. Colonel Kyle Martin was there that day. It was his leadership and the bravery of his marines that saved what little hope mankind had. When Earth was threatened with invasion, Martin again felt the weight of war pressing down on him.

Known as the Butcher of Hyderabad for his decisions in the Indian War, Martin seemed a poor choice to guard the peace but the perfect man to organize the forces of Earth to defend itself from the coming alien scourge.

With a select team of humans and a few allies among the alien races, Martin is tasked with not only defeating the invading armada, but with making sure that Earth is kept free from any alien domination.

Faced with impossible odds against an overwhelming foe with advanced technology, it is only a secret about Earth itself that gives Martin the glimmer of hope to succeed.

With his "lucky charm" Ramirez, his go-to girl Kitch, and an unshakable Sergeant Major, Martin rolls the die time after time in audacious gambles with the stakes being nothing less than the survival of the human race. Fast-paced action awaits in this military sci-fi adventure.

The Ghost of Sherwood

Behind every legend lies the truth. Behind the truth lies the lie.

Upon the sudden and violent death of King Richard, Robert Brewer fears for his future as the Sheriff of Nottingham. Knowing that King John will replace him, the scheming Sheriff decides that stealing from the rich—the King's taxes—will provide him a comfortable retirement. But when the new King, enraged over the thefts from a band of outlaws—an imaginary group invented by none other than the Sheriff himself—dispatches the cunning Sir Guy to hunt them down, the Sheriff must play both sides of a coin that takes one dangerous turn after another as Sir Guy leads him on the trail of a ghost ... the Ghost of Sherwood.

Bible Stories for Grown-ups

Bible Stories for Grown-Ups is a collection of 39 Bible stories written for adults who have little background in the Bible. These stories are told in simple, modern language to be easily understood by anyone who is interested in learning more about what is in the Bible.

From Abraham, to David, to Jesus, and Paul, these stories start at the creation of the world and go into the founding of the Christian church. Whether a first time reader or someone who just wants to refresh their memory of what the Bible holds, you will enjoy this collection of stories.

35598542R00150

Made in the USA
Lexington, KY
17 September 2014